C000054834

Towards the End

Towards the End

Joseph Mills

Polygon
EDINBURGH

© Joseph Mills 1989
Polygon
22 George Square, Edinburgh

Set in Linotron Sabon by
Polyprint, Edinburgh and
printed and bound in Great Britain by
Redwood Burn Limited, Trowbridge, Wiltshire

British Library Cataloguing in
Publication Data
Mills, Joseph
Towards the End.
I. Title
823'.914 [F]

ISBN 0 7486 6031 3

Contents

for

my mother, father, brother
Tommy, Ian
Gerry, James
Janette, Jane
Liz, Helen
Jimmy Sommerville, for the brilliant Bronski Beat and Communards
Many thanks to David Rees, Peter Robins
and Paddy Lyons for help and
encouragement, with
this book and
in general

'Maybe all there really is is just the next thing
— the next thing that happens.'
MARILYN MONROE
The Misfits

A Black-hearted Satanic Cupid
Sets Things in Motion

Although it was a cold dark January when I first met Alex, the seeds of our relationship were planted six months earlier. It was then that I began to will him into being. It was then that the years of frustration and yearning finally became unendurable and I let it be known — like a latterday Dr Faustus — that I was desperate, unhappy and reckless enough to enter into any pact for some sort of peace of mind.

It was the last day of term: that's why what happened was so frustrating — like the first appearance of the sun on the final day of a dreary holiday, although the years I spent at St James High School were anything but a holiday, even a dreary one. I had no intention of attending the fifth form end-of-term dance; the only reason I went was because Maurice Burns — the one close friend I'd made at St James — was going, so I suppose I have him to thank, although I was anything but happy with him at the time. Neither of us had ever attended a school dance before, and the fact that he no longer seemed to share my disdain for such events appeared to me to be yet another indicator of our accelerating drift apart.

The venue for the dance was the Assembly Hall of St James, which was ludicrously over-heated, following complaints about the temperature at the Christmas dance. Despite the heat, the fifth-formers were steadfastly refusing to peel off any layers of their weekend clothing as they strutted about in wildly-coloured ensembles, the boys' sparkle and flash easily matching the girls' in the swaying, jostling crowd which, trapped beneath the pulsating disco lights, glimmered and changed shape like a chemical reaction.

Although alcohol was forbidden at the disco, several students had managed to smuggle something in. Some were already drunk, swigging from bottles of strong German beer on the dance floor, as those around them ducked and dipped to avoid the amber projectiles' jagged circuits through the air. Some of the more careful boys — the ones who were in love, dancing slowly with their girlfriends, eye to eye, smile to smile — glanced nervously at the extroverts and then at the doors: but they needn't have bothered. The last brave teacher had long before been driven away by the loudness of the music, the glare of the lights.

It wasn't only the boys who were becoming drunk: already several girls had danced past me with unmistakably solicitous smiles. I could see a group of them by one of the fire exits giggling and pointing at me and any other unattached males in their vicinity. Maurice was on the dance floor, shuffling away contentedly with a girl from his French class. I began to move towards the quieter end of the hall. Multi-coloured strobes were stuttering in time to the music as I wove my way through the crowd: red, blue and green faces appeared and disappeared like flashing fireworks; the ugly frown burned onto my retina for a black half-second was immediately replaced by a sexy smile, a statuesque profile, an eyebrow swept by dishevelled blonde hair: desire and contentment, modesty and conceit, beginnings and endings were all revealed and magnified in the gaudy frozen expressions. The Disc Jockey gave us some banal advice about watching our tummies, as though he thought he was at a children's party, and was promptly shouted down by a chorus of FUCK OFF! 'Who is that moron?' and MOTORHEAD YA BAS!

When I reached the other side of the hall I found a quiet little table with a few plates of cakes and biscuits on it, reminding me that I had hardly eaten anything, in my nervousness, since I left the house. I ate standing against the table, mesmerised by the strobes which brought to mind all those boring physics problems I'd had to endure throughout the year. The boys had at last begun to shed some of their layers of clothes, following the lead set by Billy, the weight-training fanatic, who was already down to his skimpy blue shorts, which were so insubstantial that a mass of black pubic hairs peeked out indecently over the waistband. And there was Brian from English Lit, smoking a cigar, an attempt to live up to the reputation for individuality he had earned the day he came into class and sat on the floor in the space where his chair should have been, when he found that it was missing.

The strobes suddenly stopped and the hall burned with lascivious red as Lionel Ritchie sweetly signalled the start of the slow dances. The dance floor immediately half-emptied as those without a partner daring or devoted enough to stay up made a mad dash from the centre of the hall, and scattered against the walls. The lucky ones still left on the dance floor smiled as their friends pointed and laughed from the side in an attempt to conceal their jealousy. Through a space in the crowd, I suddenly became aware that I was staring at something unusual: two boys, one blond, the other dark-haired; the blond was talking to a girl, drink in hand, while the dark-haired friend stood behind him, arms clasped around his waist, head turned sideways, resting against the blond's back as he licked at his ear. I wondered if this was just another manifestation of that drunken male physical camaraderie I'd seen so much of. As if in reply to my unspoken query the dark-haired boy lifted his head from the blond's back and kissed him on the cheek. The warm red light was replaced by blinding silver.

It was Jim Forsythe and Walter Murphy.

I never let them out of my sight for the rest of the night, but they seemed determined to do nothing that would distinguish them from the other boys. They smiled a lot at each other and talked a lot; sometimes they danced

with girls in their company, sometimes with each other —
but that was not unusual by the end of the night when
other pairs of boys were dancing together to records they
had requested, and those who were going to score had
already done so. Could what I had seen have been simply
playfulness — or my own imagination? I closed my eyes and
conjured up the image again, but already I was embellishing
the memory: tightening Jim's grip, prolonging the kiss on
the cheek.

I lost sight of Jim and Walter when the disco finished and
we all filed out to await the coaches that were provided to
take us back home.

As I made my way to the exit, Brian, the school joker,
stuck a wet contraceptive in my hand and said, 'You need
these more than we do now, don't you?' I continued to
weave my way through the crowd, smiling haughtily as
I watched him swagger off into the crowd. Finding the
direction he had headed off into blocked, he had to retrace
his steps back through the crowd towards me.

'I'm getting a great new calculator for next year,' he said
to me when he found himself by my side again, cheeks pink
with embarrassment after his prank.

Brian was one of the boys who had harassed Maurice
and me in earlier years. Considerably more mature in fifth
year, he seemed to be trying to make amends by awkward
attempts at indicating friendship — like sticking a wet
contraceptive in my hand, or asking me to help him with his
maths homework. Like many of the slower boys who wanted
to improve their academic performance, Brian spent more
time buying expensive calculators, stationery and self-help
books than actually getting down to the work itself, like
a nervous sculptor, constantly sharpening his instruments
in order to delay the moment when work would have to
begin.

'What was wrong with the old calculator?' I asked as
we squeezed through the crowd, his spiky hair tickling my
ears. 'A calculator won't get you a Higher maths you know.
Your trouble is —'

'— that I go all around the subject. I know. You've told
me before.'

4

When we got outside he made his way over to a group of friends and became the joker again: 'Can I have my rubber back — or are you actually considering using it?'

'No — I think I'll hang onto it,' I said. 'I'm sure it'll come in handy for something: there are so many things you can do with rubber, aren't there?'

I went over to the bus shelter to await the coach that would carry me back to the countryside village I'd loathed ever since my parents had wrenched me from the city to live there, with its gardens and gnomes and strange dialect I'd never adapted to. Jim and Walter would be waiting for the bus going in the opposite direction — to Glasgow, the Big City I longed to return to.

I leaned against the flimsy wall of the bus shelter, hypnotized by the comforting throb of rain, watching a single drop of water slowly wind its way down the glass window opposite. Argumentative voices became distinct close by, competing with the gurgling puddles.

Jim and Walter again. Questions: When? How? Why? Walter, although he was the smaller of the two, seemed to have the upper hand in the row. At least it was he who was calmer; quietly, confidently defensive. Jim's shrieks became louder and louder as he became more red-faced and out of control.

Then the balance instantly shifted — the instant that Jim caught sight of me in the bus shelter that Walter had been backing into to avoid the curious attention of passers-by. Jim gradually calmed down as he glanced over at me periodically, each glance longer and warmer than the one which preceded it. Walter, when he eventually realised what was happening, instantly shot out of the shelter and headed for the Glasgow bus. Jim smiled over at me again as he too, slowly, left the shelter. I nodded back.

When the bus finally arrived I went straight to the back. Brian had got on first and was already asleep on the back seat, his long legs curled up to make an acute angle with the rest of his body. I sat myself in the seat in front and wondered about Jim Forsythe and Walter Murphy. I felt utterly confounded, like the detective whose investigations are blown off track by startling new evidence from an unexpected source. I had been permanently on the look-out for the signs: a prolonged glance, a careless gesture, an ambiguous comment. Why hadn't those two come to my attention before now?

Jim and Walter: I had known them for four years. As far as I could remember they had made no more impression on me than any of the other better-than-average-looking boys I had shared classes with throughout the years. Now that I began to survey my memories critically though, as if I were studying in detail a photograph I'd only ever glanced at before, I began to revise my judgement.

They were both in the football team and both runners for the school. I remembered that Walter was extremely exuberant in the dressing room, always eager to get involved in any commotion that broke out; but then it occurred to me that he was prone to hysteria at any time. A memory came to mind of Walter outside a class waiting to get in, enthusing about some pop record that was in the charts at the time. I recalled his choice of words when talking about his tastes in music: love, adore, idolize, and it suddenly struck me that something about his ecstasy had caught my attention at the time: why otherwise would the memory have survived for so long?

Jim I had even more memories of. It was a surprise to me when I remembered how many times we had had conversations together: his interest in my tastes in music and his invitations to play table tennis when he brought his little portable set in on end-of-term days must have seemed at the time simply manifestations of his boisterous friendliness, but I saw them now in a different light.

The bus pulled into Woodhaven. A pale half moon lit the pristine gardens and the gnomes which were freshly painted every year, as carefully and painstakingly as a model's face. Jim and Walter would be cavorting through Glasgow's neon vitality, making up. It would be six weeks before the beginning of the next term. All those days and nights before I could grasp at the lifeline that I hoped had been thrown at me.

Trapped. Wanting to hold and be held. A mental howl of anguish. Somewhere the ears of a black-hearted satanic cupid prick up.

There is no such thing as love at first sight. Who you are before you first set eyes on the object of love — your receptiveness to love in general, any lover in particular — is just as important as the qualities of the lover. That is why what happened between Jim and me is so important to my time with Alex.

By the time the new school year began I was almost hysterical with expectation. It would have seemed impossible on those cold, dark mornings during the school term, when the alarm seemed to go off ten minutes after I'd drifted off into sleep, to imagine that there could ever be anything better than not having to get up to go to school; but every year, as predictable and unexpected as death, there came the boredom and aimlessness of the holiday weeks: the exasperation with my mother's bland daily routine, and the avoidance of her, lest I should become embroiled in it; the re-re-reading of old books and magazines; the three times a day masturbation sessions; and the attempts at trying to trick myself psychologically into believing that the hours between meals were becoming shorter. All this free time I spent fantasising about what would happen next term.

I believed there was one answer to a set of different problems: I was gay, lonely. Jim and Walter seemed to be a happy, balanced gay couple. I would speak to them and they would tell me where to go, what to do, and the problem would be solved. So I believed anyway, as I whistled away on the bus to St James that first day.

As usual the weather began to improve as the summer holidays came to an end. That first day back seemed to be the hottest of the summer. Even at nine in the morning the sun was so bright that it was impossible to look at it straight on as it beamed down onto the playground like a cosmic flashlight. Several second-year boys were taking the opportunity to burn their names onto their brand new briefcases with magnifying glasses. Most of the names were indecipherable, but the boys who were good at it got so carried away that their briefcases ended up covered with the engraved names of pop groups and sports heroes.

The first-year boys, crowded together like tiny tailor's dummies, were too sick with nervousness to play like the other boys. They used up most of their energy avoiding the attentions of the older boys who were mocking their pristine uniforms and frightening them with apocryphal tales of rules and customs at St James. I paid little attention to the younger pupils: I was more interested in the fourth and fifth-years who were obligingly performing provocative stripteases as the heat increased and we waited for classes to begin. So, it seemed, was Jim Forsythe. He was seated next to a large pile of school jackets which were huddled together fraternally on the dusty playground, as unself-conscious about their slovenliness as their owners were. Ties were yanked off and thrust into pockets or tied around wet brows; unbuttoned shirts hung sloppily over trouser belts and jackets and ties were eventually transformed into goalposts and whips.

All the time Jim's head had been darting about, like mine, following the sweaty muscular movements of the boys. But even when the pupils began to be let into the classrooms his head was still darting about: as though he were looking for somebody.

That afternoon I discovered we were both in the same class for history — McIntyre's, the school alcoholic.

He arrived twenty minutes late without books or notes and began to drone on about Disraeli, going into far more detail than was necessary, and drawing intricate, largely irrelevant maps on the board. He made no attempt to disguise his boredom with the subject, taking every opportunity to digress: when Greece came into the lesson we were subjected to a long, tedious report of his recent holiday there. When that story was over he began to ask the class questions, trying to prove that his old pupils were better than anyone else. Somehow he always managed to pick out the real dunces: one of them didn't even know who Castlereagh was, but McIntyre enlightened him.

'Castlereagh was Canning's predecessor as British Foreign Secretary. A great European, he represented Britain at the Congress of Vienna in 1815.' This time-wasting monologue ended with 'By the way, Castlereagh was a raving poofter — but you don't need to know that for the exam.'

It was while looking round the classroom to gauge the individual reactions of the pupils to this great witticism that I noticed Jim sitting up the back. He seemed not to be laughing or smiling but it was difficult to tell without staring.

After class I followed him to the sixth-year common room. Apart from a pool table and a dartboard, the common room also contained an old battered mono record player, a relic from the sixties which was more an object of curiosity and nostalgia than a functioning device. Jim went over to it and began to fiddle with the volume control: it was so dirty that it had to be turned this way and that, as though the user were dialling the combination of a safe, before it could be made to work. Jim managed to get it to work, but the instant he left it someone bumped into it and the sound disappeared. I smiled consolingly and stood next to him at the small counter that sold tea and coffee and chocolate biscuits. We hunted together for the least uncomfortable seat, eventually settling for the long sofa which had a table in front of it where we rested our cups of tea. I was sitting back in my seat, Jim was leaning forward over his tea as though it were a crystal ball, gazing at the circles of milk spinning round on the surface. He obviously recognized me, but I wondered if he even remembered my name: it had been a few years since we had shared any classes. Suddenly he stretched out his arms and yawned: 'I've just come from a really boring class, Paul,' he said, then leaned forward over his cup again.

'I know,' I said, 'McIntyre's history class. I was there — down the front.'

He glanced round. 'Were you there? He's useless, isn't he? I know folk who had him last year. They say he gets worse.'

I leaned forward, taking my cup out of its saucer. 'If I were you I'd be worrying,' I said. 'I had him in third year: he always dries out for the beginning of term then totally loses interest.'

'Oh, I've been reading on a bit myself during the holidays,' he said in a rather depressed tone. 'In the past few weeks anyway.'

I was trying to think of a way of bringing the conversation round to McIntyre's queer joke. It occurred to me how unusually subdued Jim was, as I watched him dipping his chocolate biscuit into his tea, letting the chocolate melt into the cup. Most of the other times I'd seen him he was bubbling with nervous energy, finding it impossible to keep his limbs motionless.

'Is Walter still at St James?' I asked in a sudden burst of inspiration. It was only when Jim's face relaxed that I realised how tense it had been.

'Yes, he is,' he said, with the relief of someone at last admitting to a lie.

'I saw both of you at the last school dance.'

He smiled, lit a cigarette, and leaned back on the settee, facing me at last. 'I don't see him anymore.' He offered me a cigarette, which I refused.

'What — not at all?' His elbow was an inch away from mine on the back of the settee.

'Not if I can help it,' he said, staring into my eyes as he spoke, the meaning of his words as hazy as the blue-grey smoke which followed them. '*My* decision,' he added, as though he had read some judgement in my eyes, 'although it was his actions that precipitated it.'

I nodded as he smiled at the preciseness of his explanation. It was, it seemed, assumed that I would understand, and I tried my best to pretend that I did.

'How's old Maurice these days?' he asked. We both smiled: Maurice was a bit of a school joke — with his acne, his weight problem and his rapidly thinning blond hair. It was his self-deprecatory humour that had attracted me to him all those years ago. But in the last year at school the campness had been toned down and we had begun to drift apart, as I explained to Jim.

'Drift apart,' he said dreamily, mulling over the words. 'Does anything really just drift apart from something else? I mean a boat doesn't just drift away from the coast: someone doesn't anchor it properly; the waves carry it away.' I was about to attempt some sort of reply to this when he suddenly asked me if I wanted another cup of tea, granting me his first unrestrained smile of the day. I accepted.

I watched Jim as he went over to the counter: there was a lot of sensuality in his awkwardness: the clumsy lopsided walk, the rough, irritable fumbling in his pockets for change, the appealingly untidy brown hair and the way he hunched his shoulders up and scratched his head as he asked for two teas and a box of matches.

'What about you?' he said when he returned. 'Are you seeing anyone?'

I hadn't a clue what to say. I felt the foolish, helpless panic I had felt halfway through last year's oral French exam when the examiner had said something totally unintelligible to me. Did he mean boys or girls? If he meant girls then I was totally wrong about him and making a fool of myself. If he meant boys then he was crediting me with a lifestyle I had no experience or knowledge of.

'No. Not yet,' was all I could think of to say. I was vaguely aware that the room was emptying.

'I've never seen you around much,' Jim said, flicking ash onto the floor. 'Do you go out often?'

'Around' 'Out' 'Anyone' — everything he said was so ambiguous. This was probably intentional: he must have been as unsure of me as I was of him. 'No — I've been trying to get ahead of things, like you,' I said, hoping to drag the conversation onto more familiar ground. 'That takes up all my time at the moment.'

We both silently finished off our tea. I sat back in my seat, my head beginning to ache, wishing I was on the bus home, going over the conversation carefully at my own speed.

Jim leaned back also, again facing me, his elbow very lightly, but very definitely, touching mine for the first time. 'You should get out every now and then,' he said. 'You can't study all the time.' I nodded and he asked, 'Do you want to go into Glasgow next Friday?'

'Okay,' I said, much too quickly I realised, so I added, 'Friday . . . Yes, that should be alright.'

Jim put out his cigarette and stood up. 'I'll meet you here, Friday at dinnertime then, and we'll make arrangements.'

'Thanks for the tea,' I said as he walked away. He turned back and smiled.

By the time I got home that night I was exhausted, having analysed the conversation over and over throughout the remainder of the afternoon and on the bus on the way home. I told myself that this was necessary: it was the minutest details that mattered — had he said 'Are *you* seeing anyone' or 'Are you *seeing* anyone?' The prospect of the meeting on Friday terrified me — especially if we had been talking about what I hoped we were. I was convinced that I, still a virgin, would make an utter fool of myself with Jim, who seemed so easy and experienced.

In the end all my anxiety was unnecessary: Jim never turned up. I had set the alarm especially early, spent ages getting ready in case he wanted to go somewhere after school (my pubic hair, smothered in talcum powder, looked like a snow-covered Christmas tree). When it was obvious that he wasn't going to turn up I spent half the afternoon trying to find out what classes he was supposed to be in. Eventually I discovered that he hadn't been to any classes since the first day back. I was disappointed but relieved: he was only ill.

It was a couple of weeks later that I discovered the truth. Passing by the common room, I glanced in and saw Jim and Walter there. Jim was sitting back on the settee, his arm stretched out behind Walter, who was leaning forward over a cigarette. I marched straight over to them before I had time to consider my actions carefully.

'Together again?' I said, standing above them. Walter looked confused, but handled his confusion well, as though he was used to it. Jim was clearly embarrassed.

'For now,' he laughed, trying not to look me in the eye. 'I managed to get a transfer from McIntyre's class,' he added optimistically.

'How long's that you've been back together now?' I asked, gaining no comfort from their embarrassment, but simply curious, in the way that one is absurdly curious about the details of a tragedy: the exact time of the suicide, the make of the murder weapon.

'About two weeks now,' he said coldly, turning away: just after we'd met. I wondered if I should tell Walter that Jim and I had a date. The desire to hurt Jim in whatever way I could was overwhelming. He looked better than I'd ever seen him before, his heavy physique outlined in blue denim and white cotton, the roughness of his profile emphasised by the tenseness which was pulling down the corners of his mouth and causing his brow to furrow. When he turned and focused his black disgusted eyes on me I felt suddenly exhausted and fled the room.

I didn't allow myself to think about the incident until I got home that night, like someone hiding away the broken remains of a favourite possession until he could bear to look at them. As I lay on the bed I felt a pain I never had before: the emotional equivalent of the physical suffering I experienced the day after my first athletic class, when I had been exercising muscles I never knew existed until their presence was revealed by their aching.

I found that I couldn't think rationally about what happened, a fact which frightened me tremendously. In the past, no matter what the problem, I had always been able to break it down into little components and sort them out into a tidy logical sequence which enabled me to always find a solution — even if the solution was simply to do nothing and wait for further information. But this was a new type of problem: it refused to be broken down into handy components. My mind was full of images which defied investigation — Jim's eyes, Walter's bewilderment, Jim's sexiness, Jim's roughness, Jim's profile, Jim's walk. I masturbated but that only made me feel worse.

I got off the bed and set out my schoolbooks on my desk. But even as I was creasing back the pages of the exercise book and sharpening my pencil, I knew that I would get no work done that night, perhaps any night. I couldn't dismiss the fact that in such a short space of time I had become so attached to somebody. I realised how anxious I was for emotional and physical reciprocation. In the past, with no prospect of involvement, it had been easier to store up all that affection and lust and put it in the box marked 'Someday'. Now that the scent of hope had come my way, a need in me that had been for too long suppressed by logic and cynicism had risen to the forefront of my consciousness. I knew now that this need was not going to go away until it had been satisfied.

I was also beginning to see that love was not only affection and desire: it was also power. Jim showed that he didn't need me: immediately I felt more for him. I was becoming the sort of person who would fall in love with someone who fought to retain his power, with an Alex.

Black Cupid smiled as I threw my schoolbooks into the bin, and guided my eyes towards the vacancy for a bank clerk in a small town just outside Glasgow called Rosehill.

Rosehill was only slightly bigger and busier than Woodhaven: a wink of grimy pubs, grocers and banks if you bothered to look out of the bus window; half a page in a novel if you didn't — and that only if the bus stopped at all three stops. But it was One Step Closer To Glasgow. I had chosen to work in Rosehill, despite the forty-minute bus journey it entailed twice a day, because it was the nearest town to Glasgow I'd seen a suitable job vacancy in. I didn't have any time to wait for something better to come along: I needed to escape from Jim, Walter, St James immediately and do something positive about my situation. A job meant money, a place of my own eventually, escape from Woodhaven.

There was one other reason for the need for speed: my parents would never have allowed me to leave school unless I had a job to go to. I never returned to St James after the incident with Jim and Walter, but I only told my parents this after I'd been accepted for the bank. I told my mother first. She said little at the time, delaying any discussion until she had talked it over with my father — the usual routine, which I found infuriating. I gave them half an hour to discuss it while I waited upstairs in my bedroom. When I went downstairs mother was knitting a pair of blue boots for yet another expectant relative. As usual, when I was confronted with the subject of marriage or babies I felt as though a crime had been committed for which I knew I would take the blame, but which had nothing to do with me.

My father was staring at the television set. The sound was turned down: dumb detective dodged silent bullets. The blandness of their lifestyle appalled me. She knitted, read westerns and bought records; he worked, read science fiction and watched TV. It never seemed to have occurred to them that they could have shared interests. They seemed to have no discernible reason for living together. The way they hardly looked at each other when they spoke was frightening: they displayed the strained politeness of two people caught on the same boring train journey — for life.

'Have you spoken to the headmaster about your decision?' my father asked me at last. None of us were fond of dramatic scenes so the discussion had begun in an off-hand manner in the kitchen — a neutral zone between my territory (the bedroom where I had been spending more and more of my time) and theirs (the living room, which had become increasingly claustrophobic to me in recent years).

'After all,' he continued, 'this could be one of the most important decisions of your life.' My father was hesitant, careful, indecisive, and mistrustful of any swift, resolute decision — especially one which he hadn't been consulted about.

'Of course I haven't spoken to the headmaster,' I said curtly. 'Do you think he's interested in the personal lives of every pupil in the school?'

No matter how much I tried (and I tried very hard) I found it increasingly difficult to speak to my parents without snapping.

'Well, there must be somebody you can speak to about these things,' he said, rinsing out two perfectly clean cups which were sitting on the draining board. My mother's neurotic tidiness left inadequate props for these occasions.

'I don't need anybody to speak to me,' I said, entering the living room, 'I've already got a job. I don't want any more qualifications. I don't want to go to college yet — maybe next year.' A huge moth flew in through the living room window: Woodhaven was like one gigantic insect nest in summer.

'How about a careers officer?' my mother said, swatting at the moth. I shook my head and went back upstairs, slamming the door behind me.

The moth followed me upstairs and I swatted at it between hysterical whispers: 'I'm not going back to school because I've developed a crush on one of my classmates who rejected me for someone else and I can't bear to see *him* again and anyway I've got to get out of this glorified jungle and start living!' The moth escaped, but I felt a lot better. I lay down on the bed and dreamed about all the great things that would happen when I started work.

The office looked quite dashing from outside: polished light-coloured wooden door, shiny brass door handles and large smoked-glass window. Inside though, it was as dreary and depressing as an unemployment exchange. What wasn't sombre brown wood (the walls, the desks, the surface of the counter) was sickly pastel-coloured plastic (the custard-coloured bookcases, the pale-orange coloured chairs). Two old-fashioned black typewriters sat on desks at either side of a computer console. Huge manual calculators were set up next to petite electronic ones, looking like unfortunate deformities. All this I registered through eyes half-closed against the weak yellow fluorescent strip-lighting which radiated uncertainly from off-white tubes, cemeteries to lines of dead insects.

When I was finally let into the inner office from the customer space outside via the manager's office, I was led over to a pair of desks by the accountant, Mr Reid, who left me stranded there with the promise that he would return in a second to introduce me to the staff. I tried to make a show of disinterest in the bundles of five pound notes which the two girls at the desks nearest me were counting and separating, nervous if a stray note drifted towards me, like a naughty, neglected child. I felt like a cumbersome parcel which had been dropped in the most awkward space possible, as the rest of the staff passed by, performing elaborate acrobatic manoeuvres to avoid touching me. I longed to run out into the cool September morning: the atmosphere in the office was as clammy and oppressive as the city department stores through which my mother would drag me, leaden-footed and perspiring as a child.

It seemed to me when Mr Reid finally appeared that whole continents could have drifted apart in the time he'd been away, but in fact he'd only been gone ten minutes.

'All set for the magical mystery tour then?' he said as he proceeded to introduce 'Mr Paul Robinson' to the rest of the staff. It wasn't long before their personalities and idiosyncrasies became well known to me, but during that first round of introductions the only members of staff who distinguished themselves were Ann, the previous junior, because she would be working with me for the first few weeks, and Mary, the grade three, who added sarcastically to Mr Reid's long-winded description of her duties 'and any other dirty work that nobody else is daft enough to do'.

'Aye, Mary's a good worker,' Mr Reid said, patting the back of her chair, a remark that caused those who heard it to trade silent glances of indignation before ostentatiously speeding up the pace of their work.

When I finally stepped out of the office at dinnertime that first day, I felt as though I was only then exhaling the breath I had dramatically inhaled as I rang the doorbell for the first time. Only when I was out of sight of the other members of staff who had left at the same time I did, did I begin to feel that I was becoming a complete individual again; it was as though my personality, which had been evaporating into the dry atmosphere was now starting to seep back into me. This sensation only diminished slightly as the months passed and summer gave way to winter.

The bank became more bearable to work in, almost romantic, as the nights grew shorter and our little office glowed like a candle in the darkness that engulfed the town in the afternoon. The day before the bank was to close for the Christmas holiday I opened the door and an invigorating gust of winter air rushed into and circled the office. I slipped outside for a second, allowing myself one huge gulp of cold air, then I dashed back in again when Lex, the butcher's assistant, strode past me into the bank:

17

I wanted to make sure that I dealt with his deposit account book.

The best thing about a Friday was that it was the day Lex brought the butcher shop pay-in to the bank. He was two years younger than me, but a foot and a half taller, with the deepest blue eyes and the fairest skin, which glowed red with the winter chill. His steady, good-natured smile and solid footballer's legs always seemed to carry him to the front of the queue and out again quicker than I would have liked. Undoubtedly his quick exit from the bank was helped by the plastic bag of left-overs he carried home from the butcher's to his mother's every week.

'Three pigs' elbows and a rabbit's brain,' he invariably answered to anyone asking for a description of the contents of the bag of red meat, which always looked obscenely alive. He revelled in their squeamishness, his coarse laughter and enormous frame reducing the small office to the size of a doll's house, and my hand to the size of a doll's when I handed him back his bankbook, delighted if a drop of blood fell from his hand to mine.

'Cheers mate,' he said that day, giving me the benefit of his wide laughing smile which ended up a neighbourly wink. He probably forgot my existence the second he turned to go, in the same way that I forgot the girls who managed to conduct a skimpy flirtation in the five seconds it took to hand over a bankbook.

'Have you ever thought seriously about marriage, Paul?' Ann asked me in the tearoom later that day: we still took the same teabreak even though we no longer worked together. She was reading *Cosmopolitan* or *Orgasm Monthly*, something like that.

'It says here that although most people today believe that marriage is on the decline they're wrong: it's actually more popular than ever.'

'How do they make that out?' I mumbled, without lifting my eyes from the paper I was reading. Recently I had enjoyed my conversations with Ann less and less. During the first few weeks, when we indulged in deep discussion every time we were alone, I enjoyed her revelations about her anxieties over her mother's health and her hopes and dreams for the future. But after a while it became obvious that her story was not told for free: she was offering it only in exchange for my own.

'Well, it says that although one in three marriages ends in divorce,' she replied patiently, 'most divorcees remarry.'

'Some people never learn, do they?' I said, looking up at her. 'I think I'll just not bother getting married and save myself the bother of having to get divorced.'

Ann suddenly leaned over the table and put her hand up to my face. 'You've got something in your eye,' she said, pulling my right eyelid down.

'Oh, just leave it, Ann,' I said, actually quite enjoying the attention. 'If I can't feel it, it can't do me any harm, can it?'

I knew that Ann found me attractive, but I took little pride in her interest, realising that it was only attraction by default — all the other male members of staff were either married, too old, or had girlfriends. The more I ignored her obvious interest in me, though, the more determined she seemed to be to express it.

'Just because you can't feel something,' she said, suddenly pulling my eyelid down painfully, 'doesn't mean it can't do you any harm.'

'Ouch,' I said unemotionally, abandoning my paper.

'Oh, so you do have feelings,' she said, loosening her grip on my eyelid.

I wondered what the limit of Ann's imagination was when she thought about me. My own fantasies were only specific and detailed when they were sexual: any romantic dreams I nurtured were abstract and vague. Beyond discovering the mystery contained within the butcher's apprentice's baggy overalls my mind was usually too exhausted to wander. Did Ann size me up physically the way I did in front of the mirror: face — almost handsome, but nose too long; hair — drab brown, but it could always be dyed or streaked; body — too slim, but it could be worked on with weights. Or was Ann considering how I would measure up as a future husband and father? If her fantasies were more concrete than my own then she was, to my mind, unromantically practical: I only wanted my fantasy figures to love me as I loved them — the details of our life together would surely fall into place naturally from then on.

'Do you mean not get married and just live with somebody, or not get married so you can sleep around?' Ann said, placing her magazine in front of me, opened at an article on young people and AIDS.

'Ann, I'm depressed enough,' I said. 'I'll cross that bridge when I come to it.'

She grinned: Ha! Still a virgin. I frowned: the second shift — Moira, Beeny, Rose — came into the tearoom.

'Right — is that all the July's?' Moira said when the girls were all settled at the table; her pen was poised over a sheet of paper as though she were a forewoman of a jury. The girls nodded and she ticked off July on the little unofficial holiday sheet which the staff prepared each year. Mr Reid would circulate the official sheet round the office in February, but by then the staff had worked out their own programme which took into account the two or three weeks a year we were all planning to take off 'sick'.

'Wait a minute,' Rose said. 'Doreen always takes a week off in July.'

'Isn't it the beginning of August usually?' Moira said pleadingly, studying the neatness of her little table.

'Sometimes it's the end of July,' Rose said.

Moira sighed and folded up the list. 'If you're going out to the shops,' she said to me as I got up to go, 'will you get me something for afternoon tea?'

'What would you like?' I said encouragingly.

'Something fattening.'

'A strawberry tart?'

'The very thing.'

'Oh, get me one as well,' Beeny said in resignation, fishing out money from her purse. 'I'm sick of cucumbers and lettuce.' Pre-Christmas diets were in fashion, but it was only the slimmest girls who stuck rigidly to a regime: the really plump ones like Moira and Beeny ate their diet dinner (minutely cut salad sandwiches and half a grapefruit) then sent out for something else to eat, alternating cream cakes with cottage cheese.

'Oh, did you see Dallas last night?' Rose said with sudden delight, as though she had just remembered a box of chocolates she had in her bag. The other women smiled in anticipation, as though the chocolates had begun to make their way around the room.

Outside in the office Mary was moaning indignantly to one of the customers, her dark tangled hair becoming more and more untidy as she bobbed her head about, mouth snarling, spitting out the various injustices she had suffered throughout her years in the bank. The woman she was speaking to, like all her victims, was happy at first to be privy to behind-the-counter gossip, but soon grew weary at the force of her venom. She had to hurry, I heard her say: she'd left her dog outside and it was a wanderer. Mary was in one of her moods; there would be an argument later in the day: good. The tantrums, arguments, machinery breakdown — any change in the drab routine — were the only things that made office-life bearable.

It wasn't working out: three months of drudgery and nothing to show for it. I was just as frustrated as ever — only now I had Lex and the other attractive customers to lust after rather than Jim and the pupils at St James.

When I went into the tearoom to get my coat at the end of the day, Ann's magazine was still lying open on the table at the AIDS article. 'Time Is Running Out' was splashed across the two pages. I copied down one of the gay contact numbers beneath it.

As I walked to the bus stop the euphoria I felt at my decision to make a move at last was slowly being dampened as I passed yet again the monotonous row of shops I was already too familiar with: Dalziels (pronounced Dee Els), the bakers where I got the staff tea things in the morning; Stewarts, the newsagent's where I got my music papers every week; Orr, the butcher's shop with the sexy assistant; and Halperns, the most depressing shop on the street. On either side of the name of the owner was painted in red italics (sixties style) 'clothier' and 'costumier'. The display in the window was the exact same one I had viewed on numerous bus journeys through Rosehill over the years: an olive-coloured mannequin wearing a thin white dress, looking pale and sickly in the alien turquoise light. I couldn't imagine what sort of mentality would open up a clothes shop in such a small town, twenty minutes from Glasgow.

At the bus stop I began to notice the cold, was exhilarated by its impersonal caress on my skin, like an accidental collision with a handsome stranger. I gulped deep breaths and my mind became clearer with every sting in the lungs. Gradually I was beginning to lose the self-induced sleep-walking state I let my mind and body succumb to when working in the bank. The bus eventually came — ten minutes late — and for the fifty-ninth time (if only I hadn't started counting), I began the journey from Rosehill to Woodhaven.

On the way out, Mr Reid had announced that there would be a new grade four joining the bank after the holiday: twenty-six and married — a lot of good he would be to me.

A black-hearted satanic cupid smiled and moved on: all was going according to plan. He was no longer needed here.

Infatuation

Alex Anderson was taller than any of the other members of staff except Mary. His face could not be labelled handsome unequivocably, largely due to the fact that it was so responsive to his moods that it was difficult to pin one description onto it. When he was happy and talkative he looked young and pink and healthy: at his best he burned with the lascivious confident sensuality of a young labourer in the street, eyeing up the passing girls. When he turned up for work quiet and morose though, his sullenness scattered yellow lines across his face and he seemed much older.

There was a strange economy about the appearance of that face — as though God had given his face-makers an exhortation to rationalise the application of good looks on the day that Alex was created. As is obvious in sparsely furnished rooms, there was a balance between the plain and striking, evidence of much shifting and rearranging before a pleasant compromise was reached which, if the deficiencies were ignored, could be called beautiful. (Later I would apply this specious logic to Alex's character, blaming it for my failure to give up before pride went out the door.)

He had wide, attentive eyes, but at the expense of his nose, which was rather small, and round at the end; he had a strong square jaw, but his bottom lip was fuller than average for a man, so that he had the habit of either biting over it with his top lip or licking it constantly. Later he developed the habit of pursing his lips comically, like a monkey, in the middle of a perfectly serious conversation with one of the girls, who would try her best to ignore his mockery; but despite the protestations ('Oh Alex, *stop* it'), he would hold the pose until he was rewarded with laughter.

The females understood that Alex's attitude to them was far healthier and respectful than Roy, the grade four's, whose appreciation never seemed to go beyond the physical. His seedy lust was repellent to the girls, who knew that he regarded his masculinity as superior to their femininity, no matter how much he craved it.

Roy did not like Alex, nor the attention which the girls devoted to him. On Alex's very first day in the bank, Roy broke up an argument which the girls were having over the colour of Alex's hair, which was black as ink in a bottle, but greasy, so that it shone several different colours under the weak fluorescent lights.

'It's *mostly* black,' Beeny, one of the tellers, was saying, 'but there are reddy-brown bits in it.'

'That's only reflection from the light, Beeny,' Rose, teller two, said. 'I was standing right behind him outside the door when he was waiting to get in.' She lifted her hand to pat the back of her neck. 'It's definitely black all over — I saw him in the *natural light*.'

The girls were sitting behind their telling positions, outside Mr Bentley's room. Alex probably heard the giggly debate as he chatted with the manager. I had often noted, as I waited in Mr Bentley's room for letters to be signed, that the voices outside the door, raised to compete with the typewriters, customers and computer terminal, were easily heard inside the room, which was curiously sound-proofed from the traffic outside.

Roy, already in a bad mood (he was always sour on a Monday, after a weekend with his wife), had been glancing over at the girls for some time, like a cat watching a mouse inching out of its lair, waiting for the right moment to pounce — which was, finally, Beeny's high-pitched shriek of laughter (the last utterance of a steamrollered sparrow). Roy then committed one of the most serious crimes possible in our little office: he pulled rank, upsetting the unspoken democracy of a small establishment where everyone pitched in whenever another department became overloaded. Nobody was allowed home until everybody was ready to go, so it was in all our best interests to be efficient: there was seldom any need to pull anybody up for shirking. When any such ugliness did occur, there was immediate studying of job specifications and indignant refusals of cooperation.

'Right girls, that's enough hilarity for today,' Roy said, banging his desk with a ruler for emphasis, lest the attempt to impose his authority over the others wasn't taken seriously — as was usually the case.

'We're only laughing,' Rose said, after a short, apprehensive silence. 'Are we not allowed to laugh now?'

'Not as loudly as that,' Roy said, blushing now that everybody in the office was watching and listening. 'And — and certainly not right outside Mr Bentley's room.'

Beeny slid off her seat. 'What's so special about him all of a sudden?'

Roy stood up. 'He's the manager of this bank, I'm the Grade Four, and you're a Grade Two: that's what's so special. Understand?'

The girls who had gathered round Beeny and Rose now resumed their regular positions resentfully, with the infuriatingly haphazard delay of a scrap of paper swept this way and that before it finally settles in the gutter.

'What colour would you say Roy's hair was?' Beeny said loudly, and we all contemplated the straggly brown mess which bordered his huge bald patch. The question hung unanswered in the air.

Roy wasn't the only one annoyed by the argument over Alex's hair colour. I was too. It irritated me that they had the right to discuss Alex and I didn't. I could see perfectly well that his hair was jet black and I wanted to correct those who thought it wasn't. (Look at his eyebrows or the two black lines, inverted devil's horns, at the nape of his neck.)

25

Throughout the day the feeling bothered me. I had experienced something like it before — the desire to submit to the same level of sexual speculation as the girls: was the handsome customer married, engaged, experienced, twenty-five or thirty-five? — but never with the same intensity. As the day went on I tried to rid myself of the mood by forging something concrete from the abstract uneasiness (slabs of mud are more identifiable than grains of sand). But such a process was impossible in the bank, where the constant interruptions caused the train of thought begun in the morning to be no further developed by the afternoon. All I kept thinking, over and over again, was that Alex was more mine to surmise over than the girls' — despite what they seemed to believe.

Over and over: I became aware that Alex was in my thoughts constantly with the uneasy awareness with which one recognizes that a virus has been in one's system for some time, and has been spreading quickly. When had the virus first penetrated? Was it during the girls' discussion, when Alex became a prize to be won and exhibited? Or was it earlier, when he was introduced to me for the first time?

The girls, I noted sourly, were more forthcoming with Alex when he was led around the office by Mr Reid than they had been with me. It was all coy smiles and bad jokes.

'There's still time to change your mind!' Ann said, as she shook hands with Alex.

'Aye, you could always be a basketball player,' Moira, the terminal operator, said when she turned around in her seat, lifting her head ostentatiously as she found herself only at thigh level with him.

'Ready for some hard work I hope,' Mary said briskly to Alex when she was introduced. He had been transferred chiefly to share some of the responsibility of Mary's desk: she had been gleefully unimpressed (Mary hated sharing work) when she learned that he had come from a tiny sub-office in the south-side of Glasgow.

'I hope you're an expert on Standing Orders,' she said, turning her attention back to the mass of files and computer print-outs that covered her desk. Mary thought these introductory tours were a waste of time when there was so much work to be done. Alex seemed to take an instant liking to her, if my guess was correct and his thin grin indicated fondness and his wide smile disdain.

It was only when I saw Roy and he together that I realised how impressive Alex's physique was. Roy had previously been the tallest, best built male in the office. He was extremely proud of his body which, in contrast to everything else about him, was, for a thirty-five-year-old, well preserved. Roy's desk was weighted down with sports tournaments: one for semi-pro tennis, one for swimming, and an ancient one for football, which must once have been proud silver, but was now prematurely ash-grey and wrinkled.

Alex towered over Roy in every way: apart from his superior height, he had the natural, slim, taut muscularity of a young man in his twenties; this made Roy's heavily exercised barrel chest and balloon-like shape look as pathetic and false as a middle-aged woman's pancaked face compared with a sixteen-year-old's unadorned radiance. Alex's imposing height and physique were plain to see, but the baggy, ill-fitting suit he wore (blue with black pinstripes) concealed much of the eroticism of his body from all but the most observant. The most overt sign of sexuality was the tight, round bum where the trousers cut into him when he put his hands in his pockets and the jacket came up at the back. Every time he did this, I could hear Ann's measured stamping become erratic as she focused on the blue-black curves.

Confronted with Alex's vigorous brightness, Roy's face flushed, and he stammered, in the same pitiful way he did when dealing with a gorgeous female customer. He straightened his tie and fidgeted with his baldness, unusually alert to his appearance, perhaps sensing that the superiority he had over the other males in the office (in his own eyes anyway) was over.

I was anxious to get my introduction to Alex out of the way. I wasn't getting a stroke of work done as I waited for him to reach me. All my concentration was going into making sure that I presented a favourable first impression. I hadn't a clue what Alex's attitude to office life was, so

I was trying to decide how best to put over an air of resigned contempt (a mocking smile at whatever banality Mr Reid introduced us with), while still preserving an aura of efficiency (I would return immediately to my work when the introduction was over, as if to say: well, since I'm here, I may as well try to do the job competently). I had a terrible sense, even then, of submission, of attempting to fit into whatever mould I thought would please Alex.

As I pretended to work, I watched Alex's and the accountant's reflections in the glass in front of me, edging closer and closer. Although it was, in theory, Mr Reid who was conducting the tour, I could see that, in fact, it was Alex who was dictating how long an introduction should last. When they approached someone new, Alex slowly pulled his hand out of his trouser pocket: sometimes the proffered hand lingered for what seemed a very long time before he accepted it. When he pocketed his hand again, it was a signal for Mr Reid to end the conversation and move on, which he did, probably unaware of how his authority was being subliminally subverted.

Just as they began to walk towards me Mrs Deeds came into the bank. She had a deposit account and would have come, as she did every Monday, to pay in her ten pounds. I pulled open the ledger at her account, eager to get the amendment over with quickly, in case Alex and Mr Reid passed me by. Mrs Deeds was fidgeting with her handbag. I wrote the date in the ledger. Alex and Mr Reid were almost at my side. I could smell Alex's aftershave, a cool smell like pine, which totally overpowered Mr Reid's sweet scent. I wrote in the rest of the transaction, waiting for the bankbook to be passed back for amendment: unfortunately Mrs Deeds that day decided not to refer to her deposit account. I had to score out the alteration hastily, blushing as Alex appeared at my side with Mr Reid, who was staring disapprovingly at the correction.

When we were at last introduced, I firmly shook Alex's hand which, I noted gratefully, I did not have long to wait for. To my surprise, he jolted his eyebrows up and gave a falsely curt, though warm, smile (the smile was brusque, but the eyes betrayed cordiality). It was only when he had moved on to someone else that I realised he had been imitating my own mannerism.

Maurice phoned me at home that night. I was surprised, having heard nothing from him since I left St James. We arranged to meet in the little transport café next to the school, where we had bought a snack every dinnertime to eat, while wandering around the depressing shopping centre.

'I want you to come to my sister's wedding,' Maurice said. 'Or at least my mother does.' I felt like a fake grown-up sitting in that café with the adults, discussing marriage.

'It'll be in a Protestant church,' Maurice said, eyes locked onto my hamburger. He was dieting and had only ordered tea. 'My sister's marrying a Protestant.'

'I've never been to a Protestant wedding before,' I said, pulling a chunk off my hamburger and handing it to Maurice. 'What's it like?'

'Just the same as the Catholic one, only with a shorter service,' he said, biting into the hamburger guiltily, moaning, 'Oh, I'll never get into that stupid suit my mother hired for me.'

I decided that I probably would go to the wedding, but I let Maurice ramble on about the state his mother was getting into organizing things for it: his monotonous droning was a useful background for my own thinking. As far as I was concerned there were more urgent problems to consider: didn't Maurice care about starting some sort of emotional, sexual life? Didn't he have some plan to get away too?

'We had a new guy starting at the bank today,' I told him. He was desperately trying to keep his eyes from straying towards the appetizing pictures on the café menu.

'What's he like?'

'Twenty-six — years that is.' I paused. 'His clothes were very baggy.'

Maurice continued to stare at the menu, but the firmness of his gaze indicated that the sexual innuendo had been acknowledged.

29

'He seems quite interesting,' I continued. 'Comes from Pollokshields — that's the south-side, isn't it?' I leaned forward. 'He seems to be incredibly athletic. His shoulders are enormous and his legs —'

'Hadn't we better be getting back now?'

'— are as solid as that pillar over there. Yes, I suppose we had better get going soon, Maurice. Never know what might happen if we stay out too late.'

God he was getting worse. I was gay and Maurice was gay, but neither of us had got round to admitting it to the other throughout all those long, lonely years at school. We didn't really have to: the sort of coy, camp conversations we had indulged in were admission enough. But I had become frustrated as the years went by, with Maurice's growing reticence: it always had to be me who led the conversation into the risqué areas. It was as though Maurice eagerly waited outside a safe with valuables belonging to both of us, but to which only I had the key. My resolve to let Maurice open the safe for once coincided, it seemed, with his own desire to disassociate himself from our earlier behaviour. Either way, we had been seeing much less of each other in the months up to my exit from St James.

Outside the café the sky was starless, like a huge black blanket thrown over the city. Although it was Monday, there were numerous couples around: coming out of pubs, running for taxis.

'You'll have to let me know if you're going to the wedding by the end of the week,' Maurice said. 'My mother needs to know the numbers for the meal afterwards.'

'I'll be going into town at the weekend,' I told him, in a sudden burst of inspiration. 'Why don't we meet somewhere and I can let you know?'

What could be more perfect? I needed someone to help investigate the addresses I'd got from the switchboard before Christmas but hadn't plucked up the courage to visit yet.

Knowing that such a world existed — not only in London or abroad, but in Edinburgh and Glasgow, less than twenty-five miles away — gave me a tremendous sense of peace of mind. Ironically I now felt less restless, more able to bide my time before investigating this world, as an explorer sighting an uncharted island he had been searching for, slows his pace down as he gets nearer and nearer to it. I also experienced again the sense of apprehension that I had shared with my mother all those years ago when we first received the keys to the house in Woodhaven; we put off visiting it for so long, because we realised that to confirm its existence would leave us with no other excuse for our unhappiness and discontent.

'No thanks,' Maurice petulantly replied, like a prim schoolgirl refusing a cigarette. It was as though he had read my mind.

'But we always said we'd never drift apart,' I said. 'If the only reason we have for getting together is some stupid wedding then things are pretty bad.'

'Everybody says they'll keep in touch at school,' Maurice said, nervously turning back to see if his bus was coming. 'Why should the two of us keep doing things together just because we did so at school?' The ground was dangerously slippery with snowdrifts that had become hard and icy as the night progressed. Maurice was becoming more and more agitated as he twisted and turned his heavy, awkward bulk to avoid falling over.

'Don't you miss having someone to talk to?' I asked him. 'Don't you ever get lonely?' A bus came roaring up behind us. Maurice turned too quickly, slipped and fell on his knee.

'Look, do you really want to go back to those days?' he said angrily.

A passing couple sniggered at his attempts to right himself.

'I hated school — every year up until this one — all the name-calling, and being isolated from everybody else. I just want to forget all that.' I was stunned to think that Maurice had actually thought such things through.

'I'm getting on much better with everybody this year,' he said, wiping snow from his elbow. 'Nobody bothers me or calls me names — and that's the way I like it.'

But how many half-truths and downright lies are the price for that peace, I thought, although I couldn't bring myself to say it. In the bank I had my own code of conduct for coping: it would have been impossible for me to have gone out of my way to appear 'normal', but I had managed to survive without actually lying about myself, with evasive answers and stubborn silences. To my mind though, this state of affairs was only bearable because I realised that it was temporary: Maurice seemed to be content at the prospect of living permanently half a life. Or was he?

'I'll only go to the wedding if you meet me in town this weekend,' I told him as we stood at the bus stop. It was beginning to snow.

'I don't care whether you go to the wedding or not — it was my mother who asked you: she thinks you're "a nice wee boy" — probably because she hasn't seen you for three years.' He turned away so I wouldn't see him smiling. He was remembering the last time I saw his mother, at church, and our hysterical giggles when the priest read out 'Timothy's letter to Paul'. We had spent the remainder of the service imagining ever more outrageous versions of that little communication.

'If we don't meet this time then we probably never will again,' I said finally. 'Wouldn't that be a pity?'

Maurice's bus arrived at last, and he relented.

'Okay, I'll phone you up for God's sake, if it means that much to you.'

I zipped up my jacket and walked, steadily, towards my own bus stop.

Because I knew I was meeting Maurice in Glasgow at the weekend, the days before it seemed abnormally long and wearisome. As I returned to Woodhaven on the bus after the meeting with him, the amount of time which I had to endure before getting into Glasgow seemed to stretch before me like a physical object: a grey quadrangle which, if only I had the ability, I would vault over into the weekend. Those days were only made bearable by the fact that I was learning something new about Alex during each of them: Tuesday, I learned that he had no children (good); but Wednesday, he had married young (eight years ago — bad); Thursday, he was very keen on sport (bad); but Friday, the sports he was interested in were swimming, tennis, running (good — at least they weren't the macho, male-only sports). It wasn't until Friday that I had even a brief conversation with him.

It had been a frustrating week in that respect. Everytime I managed to manoeuvre myself next to Alex, somebody called me over to another part of the office, until I was almost convinced that they knew what I was doing and were deliberately taunting me.

Even the customers seemed to be in on it. One morning, just as I was about to go into the tearoom where Alex was, alone, Mrs Hathaway turned up at my window with the church collection (plastic bags full of mixed copper and silver) to pay into the church account. She knew very well the rule about pay-ins: the staff were not obliged to hold up the queue by taking time out to count bags of mixed change — but she had caused such an uproar the last time she was told this that the manager was called and she got her way. Mrs Hathaway, with her cheap imitation fur and gaudy make-up, reminded me of the sort of woman my mother felt inferior to back in the Glasgow days. So I already hated her. When Alex walked out of the tearoom, after ten minutes alone, I short-changed her pay-in by five pounds — and decided to keep on short-changing everytime she turned up with an unprepared deposit.

Although I had resolved, at the beginning of the week, to let Alex reveal his character before I committed myself to a personality in his presence, I was beginning to panic by the end of the week, fearing that he might begin to make attachments with the other members of staff and I would be left out in the cold. He had already begun to indicate a fondness for and aversion to some of the others.

With Mary, Moira and Ann he was animated and familiar; with Beeny, Rose and Roy, wary and reserved. It was the members of staff with some quirk in their nature he seemed to find most amenable.

When I entered the tearoom on Friday, Alex, who was on a different shift from me, looked at his watch and stretched his long legs and arms. Why did he always seem to get up and go just as *I* entered the room?

33

'Alex — get your big feet out of the road — you're ripping my stockings!' Beeny shouted, swinging her knees out from under the table. Alex was far too big for a tearoom which was already overcrowded. The table was far too low for him to sit up straight in his chair, so that he had to slouch down, legs stretched out stiffly in front of him, like an invalid.

'Why don't you sit outside with Roy,' Beeny said, rubbing the leg that Alex had kicked. 'That's what John and Gary do when they're on the same tea-break.'

'Och, leave him alone,' Moira said. 'The tearoom's for everybody — not just the women.' She pushed her plump frame in towards the table. 'Anyway, if we're going to start chuckin' oot the folk that take up most room then I'll be the first to get chucked.'

I was relieved that Alex, like me, never made any attempt to sit outside with Roy and the other boys: to me it was a bond between us, the first of many that I would fabricate.

'Have you been to see any more plays in Glasgow?' Ann asked me. She was reading the *Glasgow Herald* theatre page.

'No. But I'm going into Glasgow on Saturday,' I said. 'There might be one on then.' I had been to see one play in Glasgow — *The Maids* — because I heard that the author was gay. Ever since then Ann had been trying to convince herself that I was a theatre-nut like herself.

'Oh, are you interested in drama?' Alex said to me. We were standing side by side, washing our cups out.

'Well, I've enjoyed what I've seen so far,' I said. 'But I can't claim to be an enthusiast or anything.' His aftershave seemed to smell strongly all day — or did he just refresh it periodically? That would be a sign.

'I'm in a little amateur dramatics company myself,' he said, arms folded, leaning against the sink. The girls manoeuvred themselves around his legs, which were stretched out like two fallen logs, with the patient benevolence of a mother with her nuisance child.

'Oh, I know a guy who's in the Glasgow University drama group,' Ann said. I slipped into the seat which Alex had vacated, which was warm and snug. 'He's in production.'

Alex raised his eyes to the ceiling. 'Production!' he said, drawing the words out sarcastically. 'I know the type.' Then he turned to me quickly, perhaps fearing he had caused offence: 'Are you anything to do with the group?'

'Oh no,' I said, suddenly ashamed: a bank clerk! 'I haven't really investigated that side of things.'

'You should get involved,' Alex said. 'It's a great life.'

He left the tearoom, pushing back the thick, black, greasy slick of hair which sprouted out of the top of his head like an oil-well, and hung low over his forehead; as salaciously as his eyes narrowed, his lips wrinkled at the corners.

I avoided him that afternoon, finding it exhausting being in his presence, analysing his character, and acting out suitable responses to it.

Maurice and I met that weekend for lunch at a vegetarian restaurant in the West End. The lunch turned out to be a bowl of nuts and greenery which only left the stomach craving for some real food. But I could hardly blame Maurice for that: I had chosen the restaurant which, I had been informed by Gay Switchboard, was 'friendly'. I had a whole list of these ambiguous descriptions, which ran down one side of a sheet of paper, across from another list of pubs, discos and cafés that gay people frequented. The more cryptic the description was, the more it excited my interest: 'Mixed' could only mean men/women or gay/straight; but how rough was 'Rough'? And what did 'Cruisey' mean? It would have been more sensible to have made further enquiries while I was on the phone, but I didn't want to blow my cover as the tourist new to Glasgow — a story I blurted out because I was too embarrassed to admit my total inexperience.

After the meal Maurice and I drifted into the art exhibition that was taking place in a small room adjoining the restaurant. Here there was more of the atmosphere of intimacy and exclusivity that I had expected from the restaurant next door. The browsers were ninety per cent male and some of them seemed to be to be quite recklessly effeminate in speech, clothing and mannerisms, as they studied and appraised the paintings on the walls with all the fastidiousness of housewives choosing wallpaper.

After a perfunctory tour of the artwork Maurice and I queued up at two little tables that were covered with paper cups full of red and white wine.

'Red or white?' Maurice said in mock posh accent; the question echoed throughout the room as we went to stand by a wall near the door. Most of the men there seemed to know one another so that there was almost a party atmosphere in the room.

'No free food,' Maurice said, peering around the room.

'You've just had your dinner, Maurice,' I said.

'Dinner!' He drank his cup of red wine in one gulp. 'I could have made a better meal from the flowers in my mother's window-box.'

A man with a purple neck-scarf bumped into Maurice as he made his way back to the table for more wine. I wondered what Maurice made of all this. In the first few years of our friendship we had spoken almost with one voice. Now here I was with him preparing to adjust my manner and responses in a way I would never have thought possible. It worried me that I was beginning to become adept at presenting whatever responses I thought appropriate to the character I was assumed to be in any conversation.

'So everything is hunky dory at school this year then?' I asked when he returned with *four* cups of wine for us.

'Not hunky dory by any means,' he said, carefully placing two of the cups on the floor at our feet and handing one of the others to me. 'Only more bearable: I don't know why you didn't stay on — we get away with murder in sixth-year.'

'I thought it was about time I started contributing to the family funds,' I said. Maurice took another long sip of wine, peering over his cup at the crowd at the other side of the room which had suddenly burst into raucous laughter.

'My mother's been on at me all year about that. Honestly.' A familiar nasal whine began to creep into his voice: the drink was getting to him. 'I thought that parents were supposed to drive their children on to great achievements:

everybody else at school is moaning because their mothers and fathers are forcing them to stay on at school to get more qualifications — what with all the unemployment — but my mother is desperate to get me earning at the earliest opportunity.'

Maurice had been brought up, like me, in the East End of Glasgow. Unlike my family, though, he hadn't made the dream progression of all city-dwellers to a house in the country. The Burns had slid horizontally across the social scale — to an overspill housing estate on the outskirts of Glasgow almost as decrepit as the one they left. I could imagine how eagerly Mrs Burns must have been anticipating the pay-off for all those years of feeding, clothing, cleaning and healing.

'Are Jim and Walter still at St James?' I asked innocently: the wine was getting to me too. Maurice nodded, bent down to pick up another paper cup. 'Still palling around together?' Another nod.

Do they ever mention me? I wanted to ask: but I wasn't *that* drunk yet.

We stayed in the mini art gallery until there was no more wine left. Every time one of us went over to get refills, the men hovering by the tables moved away ostentatiously as we passed by to let us through. I was enjoying the fact that we were by far the youngest people in the room, and quite obviously, objects of mild speculation.

A look of panic spread across Maurice's face when he saw me consulting my watch after the last cup was drained: it was six-thirty, far later than I had supposed.

'Why don't we go somewhere else?' I suggested.

'Oh yes,' Maurice sighed with relief. 'I thought you were going to run away and leave me.' This confirmed, I felt, my suspicion that Maurice was as lonely as I was.

We walked from the West End to the centre of the city, engaged in one of those strange drunken conversations consisting of short exchanges separated by long, long pauses, as though we were speaking to each other from different planets over a telephone line with a five-minute time lapse.

It occurred to me that this was the way it had always been whenever Maurice and me were walking through Glasgow together, the conversation petering out as we began to get caught up in the atmosphere of the streets, like a cinema audience hushing for the beginning of the film.

I loved walking in the city, loathed it in the country. In place of the countryside's endless green, insects and lazy animals, the city had a network of interesting streets, each with a distinctive character. Maurice and I enjoyed the satisfying symmetry of the city, which was a grid of long streets, all parallel or at right-angles to each other. We always followed a different path from one destination to another and back, although it was never discussed which way we'd go. One simply turned a corner, the other followed.

To walk from the West End to the centre of the city is to move from one settlement to another. We left Byres Road, with its students and posh middle-class English joggers and turned into Great Western Road, which is wide, as it needs to be, to contain its Indian and Chinese restaurants, Greek kebab houses, Pakistani paper shops, American burger bars, and English delicatessens. After Charing Cross we were in Sauchiehall Street, where East and West come together for entertainment: cinemas, discos, pubs (chic *Nico's* and down-to-earth *Speakers' Corner*). Down Buchanan Street — bookshops, banks — to Argyle Street, where the big department stores take up too much room. We turned right, away from Glasgow Cross, the Barrows, Barrowfield, a different world.

I stopped outside one of the pubs on my list. 'Oh, are we here already?' Maurice said, staggering back to look at the name. '*The Waterloo*,' he slurred. 'Doesn't exactly sound posh, does it?'

'Isn't a pub what you make it?' I asked, repeating a favourite phrase of my father's. But his reply was lost in the noise coming from the jukebox as we entered.

We sat at an empty table by the cigarette machine with our drinks. I was disappointed: even for this early in the evening the pub was very empty. There was only one person working behind the bar — a woman of about fifty, chatting with the customers who were seated at the bar. There was a depressing air of sad resignation to life in the indignant, cynical tones of their conversation: they all sounded like prisoners who had admitted their guilt and were now haggling over the punishment.

'What do you think of this place then, Maurice?' I asked. I wondered if he had guessed what sort of place it was.

'A bit —' he lowered his voice as a bearded old man stumbled past us towards the cigarette machine '— a bit downmarket.'

Most of the people who entered and left the pub were unattractive, old, and working class. The only thing that labelled them as gay, I thought, was their interest in Maurice and me: it was obvious that we were the centre of attention again. We only had to laugh out loud or turn towards the bar for them all to turn and stare at us.

We had been there for almost an hour when one of the men who'd been at the bar since we came in stumbled over to our table and asked us if we would like a drink. We shook our heads vigorously.

'We're with each other,' I said hastily. Maurice stared over at me.

'He looked like Quentin Crisp,' he said.

'You're beginning to get the idea,' I replied, drunk beyond all caution by then. Maurice said nothing for five whole minutes, staring into his drink.

'Don't you think people like Quentin Crisp give . . . it all . . . a bad name?' He glanced round at the old man, who jerked his head towards us optimistically.

'How do you make that out?' I said.

'He comes across as such a sad figure,' Maurice said. 'I'd hate to be like that.'

'But *The Naked Civil Servant* was the first play about homosexuals I'd ever seen on TV,' I said. I must have been speaking too loudly, because several faces at the bar turned to stare at us again. I lowered my voice. 'All I can say is that, after I'd seen it, I felt so much more able to cope.'

It was only after I'd managed to convince Maurice that he was wrong that I realised I had, in effect, come out to him. He must have realised too, because he trotted out a list of gay books and plays that I'd never heard of, but which sounded like the names of long-lost friends who had come to join us in the warm glow of the night.

We left the pub after eight, as it began to fill up, agreeing to meet there another week, later in the evening this time, so that we wouldn't become insensibly drunk.

On the bus home, the sun seemed to linger behind me as I left Glasgow, as though it, too, felt it belonged there. As the bus approached my stop, the driver made it obvious that he wasn't going to stop, but simply slow down, expecting me to jump off. I was so drunk that the momentum of my leap caused me to career down the street, legs racing out of control, as though I were running down a steep hill. Eventually I collided with Mrs Jackson's hedge, emerging from it perfumed with the sharp, dewy stench of wet grass, a typical Woodhaven smell I'd grown to hate, but which my drunkenness allowed me — the prisoner returned from his day out, sentence almost at an end — to appreciate fully.

One day, early in March, Alex invited John out to the pub for lunch. I hadn't realised that they had been out together until they arrived back at half-past one, jackets over their shoulders, munching at bars of chocolate. As they sauntered past I felt a tightening in my throat, as though my neck had begun to turn to iron.

Over the weeks before then I had gotten into the habit of washing Alex's cup out for him at teatime. 'Just leave it to me,' I told him one day when our cups collided under the tap, and from then on it was a daily duty which created in my mind another little bond between Alex and me. The afternoon after he had been out with John, I left the cup lying on the sink, unwashed; it was still there the next morning — yesterday's dark-brown residue now grey with anxiety.

I watched Alex and John carefully throughout that afternoon but could find no sign of any special friendship developing. His manner with the younger male members of staff was exactly the same as it had been over the last two months. He seemed to find more common interest with the other boys than I did, but it always appeared to me that, more often than not, he was simply humouring them for his own amusement, rather than carrying out a serious conversation with them. With Roy he made it plain that he was mocking him: Alex was always able to trick Roy into some preposterous boast then excuse himself halfway through the conversation, so that Roy was left open-mouthed mid-boast, looking foolish and defeated.

I was worried now that I had been too cautious with Alex: in the past two months he had begun to form attachments in the office. There were always cliques and clans in the bank, the ranks of them changing daily sometimes, but Alex's arrival there had altered some of the hitherto permanent social structures quite significantly: Roy's lording it over the other boys, Mary's isolated self-sufficiency.

Alex was the only person in the building who could handle Mary. He simply refused to take her outbursts seriously. We were all astounded when, after only three weeks in the office, Alex, when confronted with one of Mary's tantrums, began to put his arm around her, like a policeman comforting a bereaved relative.

'There, there, dear, calm down,' he said consolingly. 'You'll do yourself an injury — and then what would we all do? The place would grind to a halt.' On days when he had less patience he would shout at her, 'Oh, give us all peace, Mary. We're all sick of listening to you.'

One day he actually managed to get her to stay in the tearoom for five minutes longer than the official break: 'Even martyrs have to take a rest every now and then,' he told her, hoisting her feet up onto an empty chair. The girls loved this sort of thing and used Alex to channel their grievances through to Mary. I didn't mind his becoming friendly with the girls that much, but any sign of his forming attachments with one of the boys left me feeling betrayed, although I knew I had no right to.

The day after he had been out with John, Alex stayed in the office for the first time at lunchtime. Usually he drove home to the south-side in his little Mini. I kept my nose pointed down at the magazine I was reading throughout that lunch hour, but I was still able to notice him glancing over at me every now and then.

In the afternoon we both met in the safe where I was trapped, alone, filing cheques. One of the worst things about filing in the quiet isolation of the safe was that it often led to embarrassing forced conversations with whoever else came in: if it was Roy I was subjected to a barrage of questions about my sex life; if it was the manager or accountant, banal chatter about how well I was settling in — a subject they were still making enquiries about six months after I'd joined the bank.

I didn't turn around when Alex entered the safe, but I could tell by the way the room was plunged into darkness when he stood in the doorway who it was that had come in. He had a pile of mandates with him to file, which he dropped down onto the cabinet next to me.

'You didn't wash my cup out yesterday!' he said, wagging a finger at me accusingly. 'I nearly got lynched in the tearoom when the girls discovered it!'

I said nothing and continued to file, carefully noting how many mandates he had with him, calculating for how long I could afford to be haughty. I had already decided that I had no right to be offended by his trip to the pub with John the day before: John was almost the same age as Alex — it was only natural that he should prefer his company to mine. However, despite this mental chastisement, logic proved a poor restraint on my emotions: the instant Alex walked into the safe I knew that I would find it impossible not to let him know how annoyed I was with him.

He began his filing. Without looking round, I knew that he would be stooping down to most of the files, bending his neck like an ostrich. It suddenly occurred to me that I was going to feel lonely when he left the safe. Alex was the only person in the bank whose company I preferred to what I had hitherto regarded as precious solitude.

'We were at the pub yesterday,' he said, still facing the wall behind me. Was there a sense of guilt, or at least trepidation in his voice? He stated the fact as though it were of no importance, but the fact that he mentioned it at all seemed to indicate that he realised it was of some concern to me.

'I know,' I said bluntly. Now I had committed myself to a reaction: I was immediately embarrassed by the resentment my tone suggested.

'Why aren't you going home at dinnertime these days?' I asked, surprising myself by the tone of friendly half-hearted interest I managed to put into my voice. Alex stopped filing and came over to the short cabinet next to me, adopting his characteristic pose: half-sitting, half-leaning, legs extended before him, arms folded, the sprouting oil above his brow combed back neatly in a shiny blue-black wave.

'I felt it was too much unnecessary expenditure,' he said. 'And it was taking too long to get in and out of the city at lunchtime.'

He watched me as I filed the cheques, an occupation which suddenly seemed like the lowliest, most demeaning job in the world.

'You should have come with us yesterday,' he said, as though he were chiding a younger brother for being too scared to take a ride on a seaside donkey.

'I wasn't aware you were going,' I said, banging a cabinet drawer shut.

'I told everyone I was going at twelve-thirty,' he said defensively. 'It was only a spur of the moment decision, when I heard John saying that he wasn't going home for lunch that day.' The light in the safe began to flicker. 'Ann was there — I thought she would have told you.'

'Why should she?' (Why didn't he tell me specially himself?)

'I thought you two were quite close.'

'Not at all,' I said indignantly.

'Everybody else seems to think so,' he said, smiling. 'You could do worse.'

The light wasn't flickering: it was a fly, madly hurling itself at the bulb.

'Do you like her then?' I said, abandoning any attempt now to hide my irritation. I was annoyed at Ann, whose fawning attention had helped create this fiction; with the rest of the staff for their lack of perception; and with Alex who either never realised my interest in him or, if he did, was cruelly taunting me.

43

Alex put on the monkey-face he mocked the girls with: 'She's got a nice timidity — which isn't really timidity,' he said. '*I* think anyway.' He jutted his eyebrows up in mockery of my own idiosyncrasy.

'Those eyebrows,' he said, peering over at me. 'They're like two giant caterpillars.'

'Oh thanks,' I said, rubbing imaginary insects from my brow. 'I'll have nightmares about that.' I couldn't help smiling though: it was the most intimate thing Alex had ever said to me — what I'd been waiting for.

'Don't be offended,' he said. 'I'm just jealous.'

'They're not very timid though, are they?' I said sarcastically.

Alex ignored that. 'You've got a very expressive face,' he said. 'Like an actor's.' He was staring over at me appraisingly. I didn't dare to turn to meet his eyes.

'John and I are going to the pub again tomorrow,' Alex said, straightening up. 'So you can't say you weren't told this time.'

Before I had a chance to respond, Mary came into the safe, drawing dirty looks at Alex until he drifted back to his filing. Moira then barged into the room past Mary, knocking her against the wall, and lunged down at one of the ledgers on the floor. Then she strode back out, with the ledger under her arm and a piece of paper stuck in her mouth.

'If she does that one more time!' Mary shouted, as she cautiously crept out of the safe, rubbing at her side.

'Perfect!' Alex said. 'Pure Moira.'

I appreciated the quirks in the personalities of the staff immensely now that I began to view them with the same eye for the comic that Alex had. Moira was one of the more interesting diversions: she was always in a hurry, despite her massive bulk. On her feet she was as dangerous as a hurricane, continually throwing people aside to make room for herself. The wiser, more fragile members of staff avoided her in the same way that they would avoid a mad dog.

'Well, are you coming tomorrow then?' Alex asked when he had finished his filing.

'Okay — it'll be a change, if nothing else,' I said, concealing my excitement by a shield of indifference: the only weapon I possessed.

The following day I spent an hour and a half in the bathroom before work: I felt the new atmosphere in the pub would give rise to reassessments of appearance and personality. The meeting was a total disappointment — John came along too, and the conversation never strayed far from sport or the banking courses, which Alex had completed the year before, and John was finding impossible to cope with. I found it difficult even to be polite with John as he sat there between Alex and me — especially since his excuse for being there at all was so pathetic: his mother was in hospital that week and he couldn't be bothered to cook his own lunch.

On Friday I got Alex all to myself. John was off 'sick' — probably exhaustion, I thought, from having to cope for a few days in the house by himself. When I realised that Alex and I would have the pub to ourselves I felt the guilty joy of the adulterer presented with an unhoped for opportunity to meet his partner in sin.

We went to a different bar this time: the *Black Stallion*, a small, isolated pub off the main road. It was the least popular of the pubs in Rosehill, although I couldn't think why: it was cleaner and cosier than anywhere else that I'd been to with the staff from the bank. There was lots of light-coloured wood, which was healthy looking and pleasing to touch, unlike the slush-coloured, creaky furniture in the bank; and there were dozens of amber-tinted mirrors covering the walls, which added flattering shadows to the customers' reflections, making us all feel like filmstars or models. Best of all, there was a huge jukebox, equipped with a large selection of golden oldies, which Alex and I plundered, like schoolboys stumbling on Aladdin's Cave.

'You never close your eyes anymore when I kiss your lips,' the Righteous Brothers complained as I ordered for Alex and I at the bar. I placed the cheeseburgers, two pints of lager and two packets of crisps on the table and settled

45

down in my seat, as though I were preparing myself for a gala film première: Alex and I were the stars, and the film was projected onto the mirror on the wall in front of us. I already felt more at home in those surroundings than I ever had anywhere else outside my own bedroom. Alex had never been here before and neither had I — so now it was Our Pub.

I was now the person who waited outside the safe with the mutual valuables in it: the safe to which Alex had the key. I didn't know what we were supposed to be discussing, but I did know that I didn't want it to be anything about sport or the bank.

'Tell me about amateur dramatics,' I said to Alex, after we had finished off our cheeseburgers in silence.

'Well, there's not much to tell,' he said, holding up his greasy hands from his trouser legs, like a surgeon awaiting sterilized gloves.

'Actually that's not true,' he added, laughing at the cliché he had uttered. 'I don't know why I should play it down — it's more important to me than working in the bank is.'

I handed him a paper hanky. 'I don't know about you,' he said, wiping his fingers one by one, as though he were now pulling off the invisible gloves, 'but I have absolutely no intention of making a life of the bank.'

'I agree with you entirely,' I said, gulping down lager. 'I mean, can you see either of us sitting behind a manager's chair?'

Alex lifted his glass to his lips, then burst into a fit of giggles, spraying me with lager. 'The only person I can imagine in a manager's chair is Mary!'

'Nobody would be overdrawn then!'

The barmaid smiled over at our amusement.

'All the leaves are brown and the sky is grey': the jukebox was still in a melancholy mood, unlike Alex and me. The alcohol suddenly took its first effect on me and I felt gloriously warm and tranquil: it was as though the lighting in the pub had suddenly dimmed from harsh white to cool blue — although it was, in fact, a steady pale-green glow.

'I only intend to stay on at the bank for another few months,' I told Alex.

'I've been saying that for years,' Alex said, shaking his head.

'But I'm serious,' I said, offended by his scepticism. 'I haven't started doing the bank courses or anything — hopefully I'll have enough saved soon to get a place in Glasgow to stay.'

'What will you do there?'

It was something I had given little thought to.

'Well, I've told my parents that I might try to get into a college or university — but really all I want to do is get out of the country and into an environment that doesn't leave me feeling as though I'm sleepwalking through life.'

Alex seemed strangely offended by what I'd said.

'What's so great about university,' he said indignantly. 'It's nothing but a glorified play school.'

'Of course you were at uni' for a year, weren't you?' I said, suddenly remembering the potted biography the staff were given of Alex Anderson before his arrival at the bank. It was weird remembering a time, only two months in the past, when he was no more than a name to me. I asked Alex why he had left university after the first year.

'I just got fed up with the course I was doing,' he said wearily, as though it was a well-worn subject he was going over again. 'Maybe I was too young.' He sounded irritated now. 'I don't know.' He stood up. 'It depends on the individual what they make of it, I suppose — what they want out of life.' He headed for the bar. 'At least that's what I was told when I left: nobody ever drops out of university because *it's* at fault,' he said bitterly. 'It's always the dumb student who's to blame for failing to take advantage of such a magnificent institution.'

The pub was filling up now as workers on one o'clock lunch-breaks began to stream in. I resented this invasion and scattered our jackets on the seats next to us to deter unwelcome visitors.

'The idea was,' Alex said, when he returned from the bar, 'that leaving university would give me more time for drama — but it didn't quite work out like that.'

'What happened?'

'Well, I got married for one thing,' he said. 'I needed money: Diane stayed on at university.'

So he met his future wife at university. I drank some more lager and tried to think about something else.

'Got to be there, got to beeee there!' The jukebox was becoming over-emotional again.

'Michael Jackson!' Alex said reverentially. 'God, when he was twenty-six he was a multi-millionaire, with fifteen years of success behind him!'

'I'm sure you'll catch up with him one of these days,' I comforted. I hoped Alex wasn't the type who got maudlin with two pints of lager in him.

'Well, that's what I keep telling myself,' he said sadly. At one-fifteen we convinced ourselves that we had just enough time for another round, with the same guilty eagerness with which the girls in the office convinced themselves to have 'just one last cup' at tea-break.

'We can't leave until we've heard Lay Lady Lay!' Alex said, quite reasonably.

By twenty-five past, I was only dimly aware that it was Friday and that there was a job to go back to. If Alex had suggested that we stay there all day I would have done so. I hoped at least that we could return to work late: our walking into the bank together, partners in crime, would form another bond, I thought — this time one that all the staff could see. But the stream of workers who left the pub at twenty-five past drew Alex's attention to the time, and I had to content myself with the tentative arrangement we had made to return to the pub the following Wednesday — my birthday.

When Alex opened the pub door, the sunlight outside blasted our eyes like a flashbulb. We had to navigate our way across the icy streets half-blind, gulping in cold air to clear our minds. I began to wonder whether I'd said anything stupid when I was drunk in the pub. Throughout the afternoon, as Alex and I attempted to hide the extent of our drunkenness from the others, we would smile conspiratorially at one another, and I tried to convince myself that there was something more than simply mutual satisfaction at a shared joke in his smile. But as the effects of the alcohol diminished, I became less certain and was embarrassed as we parted at the end of the day, feeling as though I had thrown myself at someone who had spurned me.

I decided on the bus home to go into Glasgow that weekend — alone. Maurice and I had been back to *The Waterloo* a few times since the first visit, but on the last occasion someone from his French class bumped into him a few seconds after we'd left the pub: since then he had been stubbornly refusing to meet me in town. I was secretly quite happy with this new development. Maurice and I had received no more than the occasional inviting glance during our return visits to the pub: it was obvious that nothing was going to happen while we were seen as a couple.

The trip was planned meticulously: I discovered that there was an early morning workers' bus which left Glasgow at four-thirty every weekday, so I decided to go into town on the Sunday. I calculated that if I was unlucky and had to return to Woodhaven, then I would go to a late-night disco and stay to the end, leaving only an hour to kill. My parents weren't too happy about the idea of my staying out all night until I told them that I was only going to a party at Maurice's. Mr Bentley, the bank manager, was harder to please: he was not the least bit happy with my calling him at home that weekend, nor with my asking for Monday off with only three days' notice. I was so annoyed with his attitude that I resolved to take a day off sick the next time I tried this sort of thing.

As I entered the pub, alone for the first time, I experienced an intoxicating and terrifying sense of dread — a fear of something happening and equally of something not happening: this sensation would soon become familiar: it had nothing to do with AIDS — I was well stocked up on the Do's and Dont's by then — sex and love were the unknowns, the potential nightmares. I also felt again that twitching of a narcissistic nerve I never knew existed until it was aroused by so many stares.

I didn't stay long in *The Waterloo*. By the time I had finished my first pint, nobody had spoken to me except a middle-aged man in a business suit, who I made the mistake of being polite with. I realised what a blunder this was when he returned from the bar with a drink for me, sat down next to me and pressed his knee against mine beneath the table. It saddened me that — even in a gay pub — this was the only way he could communicate with me.

In a corner, at the same time, voices were being raised aggressively.

'Did you insult ma pal there? Did you insult ma pal?' A pock-faced Thriller-reject was challenging a younger man beside him.

'You better apologize right now!'

The pock-faced one's friends were attempting to hold him back.

'Steph' Steph' — forget it: he's no' worth it!' But the mounting hysteria in their voices only increased his aggression, and he lunged forward at his enemy, head first, like a bull. The customers in the pub moved back in one giant wave, as though the bodies falling to the floor was a stone dropped in a pool. I stood up and let the wave carry me to the door before my friend at the table had time to notice the empty space where my leg had been pressing against his. I realised, at last, that I now knew what *rough* meant.

Somewhat shaken, but still confident, I visited another bar on my, by now slightly tattered list: *The Vintners* — cruisey. This one was split into two levels. I decided to check out downstairs first, scanning the occupants in one long sweeping look as I turned to close the door — surveying one side of the room, then completing the circle as I turned again and strode over to the bar. I blew my hands nervously, as though I were cold from outside — although, in fact, the sudden increase in temperature caused my face to flush feverishly.

My arrival in the pub caused less of a stir than it had in the other place, I noted sourly. Not all the scrutinizing gazes that were turned on me as I walked in the door followed me to the bar; by the time I had drifted over to a space by the wall, most of the occupants had recovered from my entrance and resumed their previous activities, only glancing over at me occasionally, as though I were a parcel that had just fallen off a truck, and they were wondering if it was worth investigating or not.

This bar was smaller than the previous one, and much more crowded, with, I had noted immediately, a very different type of clientele. The chatter here was all at the same level: hushed and polite, like a church congregation waiting for a service to begin. Unlike the other pub, nobody here burst into song if an old favourite came over the sound system; nobody yelled across the bar at friends entering the pub: the equivalent gestures here were simple courteous nods and waves, which were almost as imperceptible as those at an auction.

When I had first entered the pub, most of the customers had been standing or sitting alone like me, but within half an hour, the sullen figures, who I had believed I shared a timid brotherhood with, had been joined by friends, and begun to form hearty little groups, leaving me feeling self-consciously isolated and betrayed. The longer I stood there alone, drinking far too quickly (only bringing the glass to my lips so often because I felt that a moving figure looked less pathetic than one that was staring ahead like a zombie), the more I regretted the fact that Maurice wasn't there. I needed someone to talk to — not because I was in the mood for conversation, but because I wanted to prove to the others in the pub that I too could blossom into a smiling, laughing, witty creature, unlike the morose misanthrope I resembled at the time.

When I returned from a visit to the bar, I took the opportunity to stand farther up the wall I had been leaning against, positioning myself next to two reasonably attractive customers. There were, thankfully, a number of good-looking guys there — unfortunately, the best of them were grouped together in inseparable pairs, like bargain packages in a supermarket. I had hoped somehow to get drawn into a conversation, but the music that was playing — unfamiliar throbbing disco sounds which battered at the walls and floor as though caused by the exertions of some huge invisible creature attempting to escape from the room — was so loud, and the customers' speech so monotonous, that I could not make out what anyone was discussing.

The two boys I stood next to were talking with a curious air of detachment, as though the conversation were a parcel they were holding for someone out of politeness, ready to drop in an instant if need be. I was reminded of the sort of idle chatter that takes place at bus-stops, when the sense of imminency makes any lengthy discussion impractical. Also in the same way as at the bus-stop, the participants in the conversation seemed to feel it unnecessary to face each other directly when speaking, preferring to exchange the occasional nod, but for the most time, glancing around, peering at every new customer that came in the door, with the same wary eagerness with which bus-stop idlers scrutinize every new bus that emerges from the distance, unsurprised when it turns out not to be the one they are waiting for after all.

From time to time, the two boys looked round at me together, and I jolted my eyebrows up, thinking they had said something to me — but they always just as quickly turned away again to resume their conversation. I tried to convince myself that if either one of them had been alone I would have made a move to indicate my interest. Eventually the pub became so packed that it took me ten minutes to fight my way towards the bar, get served and get back, by which time my two friends were gone, their space having been taken by two older men, slightly balding, with moustaches, who were standing in almost the same poses as the other two had been.

Although the bar was so thick with bodies, people still managed to weave their way through it, from one end of the room to another, glancing furtively then moving on, or stopping to chat to a familiar face for a few minutes. I was as drunk by then as I had ever been, and was feeling wonderfully safe and comfortable as the sea of bodies forced me this way and that. It had obviously begun to rain outside: customers were straggling in with dripping raincoats and umbrellas. Their dampness brought an invigorating cloud of moisture to the clammy atmosphere.

When last orders were called, I picked up an umbrella someone had left behind and got ready to leave — intent on approaching the first good-looking guy I saw at the disco. As I pointed the umbrella at the crowd, ready to part the sea of bodies, a figure suddenly emerged and stood before me. I had noticed the blond boy moving purposefully towards me as soon as I had made it obvious I was leaving, but I was startled nevertheless when he finally appeared in front of me; however, it was a pleasant surprise, like the sight of the unexpected brilliance of the sun when the curtains are drawn in the morning — even though its brightness had been subconsciously anticipated in the laser slits of light which had seeped in through tears in the curtains.

His skin was the smooth, dark gold that people with a certain type of yellow blondness always seem to be blessed with. I guessed that he was about sixteen from the almost invisible spray of fine white hairs on his cheeks and upper lip — an untouched looking growth, which seemed to indicate that he hadn't begun shaving. He was about six inches shorter than me, but broader and thicker, with a youthful fatness around the stomach. He reminded me of the rowdy third-year boys at St James, with his tattoos on each arm, denim jacket and blond crewcut. A pleasant, unpretentious dishevelment and brusqueness distinguished him from the rest of the cautious, sterile, scrupulously clean and sweet-smelling customers. He was a comfortable rocking-chair in a waiting-room full of hard-edged benches.

'You looked very lonely standing there by yourself all night,' he said. The voice was a surprise: it had a foreign sounding rhythm to it, rising at the end of each sentence in a questioning tone.

'I don't think I've seen you here before, have I?' He spoke with an attractive hoarseness, as though he were shouting from the bottom of a well; as he spoke, his eyes widened and his hands performed an elaborate mime of what he was saying, the total effect being that of someone communicating with someone else through a bus window. His obvious nervousness put me at ease somewhat.

'No, I haven't been here before,' I said. His eyes were focused anxiously on the umbrella which I had been holding

53

upright, but now slid under my left arm, a gesture which seemed to calm him somewhat.

'And by the way –' I added. 'I wasn't lonely: I was just enjoying being drunk.'

'I'm standing over there with some friends if you want to join us,' he said, attempting to put his hands into the pockets of his jeans — which were so tight that such a gesture was impossible. The jeans, I noted when he stood back, were well worn, light blue, with sprayed patches of white at the knees and tops of the legs, and a further erotic faded patch at the right-hand side of the crotch.

I nodded and followed him over, embarrassed by the amused, expectant faces of his friends, who were smiling over at me, above the boy's head. The three men he was with were all much older than the blond skinhead who introduced himself as Patrick. Patrick was mostly silent after the introductions, while the older men questioned me; but he occasionally interjected the odd follow-up question in a hoarse, nervous bellow. When the lights were turned up in the pub I noticed that Patrick's T-shirt was white, not yellow, as I had thought. One of his friends went to the toilet and the other two drifted off to the bar to buy cigarettes and a carry-out.

'We're all going to a party if you want to come,' he said, jutting his head to the left, presumably the direction of the party.

'As long as you promise to stop shouting at me,' I said, placing my empty glass next to his on the ledge behind him.

'Sorry — just nerves, drink,' he said, looking round the pub, which was emptier but somehow seemed smaller, now that the lights were turned up.

I felt claustrophobic and anxious to leave, but it was obviously going to take some time for his friends to gather together. One of the group — the man who had gone to the toilet — was chatting to a young, effeminate-looking boy, clearly attempting to persuade him to go to the party with him. The rest of us stood at the door of the pub, staring impatiently at the man, who was himself staring into the young boy's eyes, as though he believed that he could hypnotise him into going to the party — something the

54

boy clearly had no desire to do. The boy finally managed to break away, a piece of paper stuffed into his hand with the older man's address on it, which he attempted to conceal as he passed by us through the door, as though it were a tissue, wet with tears. We all then filed out of the pub without waiting for Patrick's friend, who was making a show of finishing off his pint, in an effort to save face.

The party was to be held in the top flat of a multi-storey block in the centre of the city. At the beginning of the taxi journey, I attempted to memorize landmarks in the road in case I should want to leave the party alone, but I soon grew tired of this. I felt that as long as Patrick was there I would be all right. We were pressed close together, facing each other in the back of the taxi, my knee thrust between his short, firm legs, grazing against his crotch.

When we arrived at the flat, I was left sitting alone for some time as the others dispersed throughout the house, performing activities which were obviously routine to them. There were only half a dozen men there when we arrived; one of Patrick's friends — the one who had chatted up the boy in the pub — disappeared into the bedroom with two of them, giggling like a schoolgirl. One of the other friends was changing records and the other had disappeared into the kitchen. Pat was rolling around the floor with a huge alsatian dog, which was gnawing at his wrists, leaving scratches that were redder than the rose tattoos at the top of his elbows. The other men in the room, all over thirty, watched dog and boy with a look of patient benevolence as the two drew apart and squared off against each other, like cowboys in a western, tension mounting as they circled a rubber ball between them.

'Patch!' a young man shouted as he came into the room from the kitchen with a tray of glasses. Or was it 'Pat!'? Whatever it was, both boy and dog responded instantly, slinking away from the centre of the room — the dog into a corner, gasping and sneezing so hard that it hit its head off the floor — and Pat towards the chair next to me. The young man with the tray had curly brown hair and the robust physique of a footballer.

'That's John's affair,' Pat whispered when the man had left the room. John was the owner of the flat. I whispered back to Pat that his taste in men was better than his taste in furniture: the house seemed incredibly bare and unlived in — like a display room in a shop window. The bookcases around the electric fire only held about ten books, mostly taken from popular films, and the album rack was similarly uninspired.

'Don't worry,' Pat said, when he noticed that I was gazing critically around the room, 'there will be others on their way now from the other pubs.'

Other guests did eventually arrive and we were subjected to an embarrassingly bad drag act: two wrinkled old men dressed up as Easter bunnies — one of whom rubbed his false fanny in my face until I thought I would die of embarrassment.

'It's not like this usually,' Pat claimed guiltily.

Some of the new guests were young and attractive, but the more attractive they were, the more likely they were to be with someone else. Pat wandered off for long periods during the evening, making it clear that he didn't want to be in the way if I wanted to pair off with someone else — but he still cast anxious glances in my direction whenever someone came over to speak to me. After about an hour of this, he seemed to have decided that I wasn't interested in anybody else, and settled down into the space on the sofa next to me.

I was slumped against the back of the sofa, Pat was leaning forward, glancing round occasionally, seemingly worried about the next move. He was still wearing the faded denim jacket from the pub which looked so right on him, the way denim does with some people. I was by this time relaxed almost to the point of unconsciousness with all the drink I'd consumed, but Pat still seemed very tense; his movements were sharp and jerky, like a character in a nineteen-twenties film, as he leaned forward, clutching his glass with both tiny pink hands, like a baby.

When he moved back in his seat to let someone pass, I put my right arm on the back of the sofa behind him, letting it fall onto his shoulder before he had a chance to sit forward. He instantly flopped back into my arm with a sigh of relief, turned towards me and kissed me on the lips, holding my face with both hands, as he had held the glass, which slid to the floor when I touched him.

I placed my other hand on his side, beneath the denim jacket. His body was as hot as a furnace. As soon as we began kissing I immediately felt myself become hard, excited by the eagerness of his mouth. When I reopened my eyes after the kiss, Pat's face seemed suddenly huge and detailed, like an image on a film screen: his eyes were grey, his eyebrows fair and wispy, like white flames, and he had a slight reddening of the skin towards the ears.

'Is there somewhere we could go?' I whispered, self-conscious about the contorted shape we were presenting to the others. Pat stood up and held out his hand, which I accepted with embarrassment, letting it slip through my fingers as we crossed the living room. He led me into a small bedroom and we fell onto the bed.

Undressed, Pat looked more imposing than he had with his clothes on: although shorter than me overall, his torso was longer than mine, smooth all over, and square-shaped. He was wearing boxer shorts with a crazy psychedelic pattern, which clung to the contours of his body as tightly as had the blue jeans he had just unpeeled from his legs. I reached down to run my lips along the firm, hot tube coiled up beneath the thin, velvety fabric. 'Fantasy of mine,' I whispered shyly to Pat who had begun to roll the shorts down before I stopped him with my mouth.

There was a weird sensation of familiarity about this novel event for me: I had fantasised about these things for such a long time — kissing, undressing, licking nipples, sucking a cock through those very same boxer shorts I'd seen hunky young guys buying in department stores the previous summer: acting out the fantasies now was like seeing the film version of a book I'd read over and over again.

The sensations I hadn't expected gave me more pleasure: I couldn't get over the fact that I was actually feeling muscles and skin that I had hitherto only looked at — the two experiences turned out, surprisingly, to be so very different — like visiting a country you'd only ever seen on television. I felt as though I had developed some new sixth sense. I had never imagined that a boy, a body, a muscle could be so firm and hard, having only, until then, my own slim frame to go by. As I ran my hands over Pat's body, from scratchy blond head to shoulders, sweaty smooth chest and baby-fat stomach, testing the hardness all over, I felt the way a newly sighted blind man must do, astonished at the gap between the two senses of sight and touch.

After I finally allowed Pat to roll down his shorts we rubbed together for some time until there came a moment of uncertainty; now and then I felt a finger stray towards my anus, but I manoeuvred it away. Just before I knew I was about to come I asked Pat to slip his denim jacket back on.

'Another fantasy,' I whispered. He smiled wildly and slipped it on.

'Roll up the sleeves — like you were in the pub.' He rolled up the sleeves until both rose tattoos were visible on each arm. I was rubbing away wildly at myself and moved closer to Pat so that I could smell the denim, and the sweat and the blondness; more rubbing, wilder — then the explosion, which I saw before I felt, due to the alcohol-numbness. But it was a huge relief, after all those years, nevertheless.

For most of the night I lay with my arms around Pat, finding it difficult to sleep, as thoughts ricocheted around in my mind, like steel balls in a bagatelle board. I went over the events of the night repeatedly, replaying the best moments over and over, like a child listening to a favourite story. I was already willing myself to forget the boring parts of the evening, shaping the night into a story to tell Maurice. It seemed such a momentous event that I felt it would only finally become reality after I had told someone else about it.

Pat had long before drifted off to sleep, like the baby he wasn't. In fact he was two years older than me, he told me, and had been going with a guy for three years before they split up earlier in the year.

In the morning I awoke to find him fully dressed, standing at the window staring out over the city. The window was opaque with condensation, except where Pat had created a forlorn, moonlike circle, already cratered with new condensation. His chin rested on his folded arms as he leaned against the window ledge. When I was dressed I went over to the window beside him, surprised, when I looked out, at how far I could see: I hadn't realised how high up we were. I could just about make out the blue face of the tall Trongate clock in the distance. Pat pointed to a cluster of houses to the east, next to a huge factory which was puffing black smoke into the atmosphere aggressively and unapologetically, like an old man at a funeral.

'See that house there?' he said, 'the one with the green bit on the roof?' I couldn't distinguish one house from another but I nodded. 'That's where I stay,' he said, with the calm resignation of a criminal pointing at the murder weapon.

Breakfast sounds drifted in from a room next door: clanking cutlery, radio banality, hangover whispers — exaggeratedly hoarse — and the smell of jam and toast and fried ham.

'Let's just go,' said Pat. 'They'll only embarrass us.'

So we slipped away, shyly.

Pat was tense again as we walked along the road and he told me what bus would take me towards my own bus station at the other end of the city centre. We were both fumbling for the best way to make another arrangement to meet each other, when my bus suddenly came up behind us and I had to run for it, parting from Pat with an embarrassed 'See you again in town then?'

At home, when the euphoria of the night before began to wear off, my thoughts began to wander back to Alex. I looked at the clock continuously: 1.15 — were Alex and John in the pub now? Or would John still be off work? Would Alex have found someone else to go to the pub with? Ann, perhaps — with her innocence which wasn't really innocence. Would they go to our pub, sit in our seats?

The following day when I returned to work I received an unexpected surprise, like breakfast in bed.

'Oh there he is now!' Moira shouted as I passed her in the office on the way in to work. 'You had your pal worried sick there — he thought you were ill or something.' She pointed to Alex, who was feigning ignorance, obviously embarrassed at Moira's revelation (and exaggeration, no doubt) of his interest in my absence.

'Well, did you miss me?' I felt brave enough to say, slapping his back, so elated was I about his concern.

Alex turned around slowly, apparently distracted. 'Well, I noticed you weren't there, if that's what you mean,' he said sarcastically.

Why couldn't he just say something unambiguously positive?

'I certainly didn't have to keep up with anyone's drinking.'

So he went to the pub alone.

We returned to the *Black Stallion* at lunchtime again that day.

'Jake's got hiccups,' Alex observed when we entered the pub to the sound of a jukebox record stuck in a groove. We had christened the jukebox Jake that first day, having come to think of it as another customer, with its happy and sad songs or its silences — which we attributed to Jake's particular mood at the time.

The conversation wound this way and that until eventually Alex asked me why I had been off the day before, when it was obvious that I was not going to volunteer the information.

'I didn't know you had taken a holiday — you didn't say anything on Friday,' he said. 'Did you just fancy a long weekend?'

'Well,' I lied, 'I was going to be in town for a party on Sunday and I knew that I wouldn't be fit for work the next day . . .'

'Good party?'

'Extraordinarily so.'

Nod. Smile.

Jake went into one of his quiet moods, so we both took turns at cheering him up. Alex put on *Hello Goodbye* and sat down with a satisfied grin on his face. I got up next and put on *I Will Survive*. Alex put on *Beat It*. I put on *Do You Really Want to Hurt Me?* and then we ran out of change. Actually Alex did and I didn't but I felt we'd used

60

and abused old Jake enough for one day: or was it all in my imagination?

I avoided Alex for the rest of that afternoon, not willing to let him upset the delicate truce I felt we'd arrived at just yet.

I only remembered that it was my birthday the following morning when I received a card signed 'AA'. And underneath, 'Clue: Not Alcoholics Anonymous — yet' followed by two small 'X's.

Alex was off work on my birthday, and for the rest of that week. Like a master cook selecting menus for a king's dinner, I had prepared and rejected several reactions to his birthday card: surprised, reserved, amused, shocked! happy. As I entered the bank that day, I finally decided that I would simply let the expression on Alex's face dictate my reaction. Then I realised that he wasn't in the office. I became aware of this even before I passed his tidy desk, noticing immediately that the office was bereft of his early morning chatter, and the overwhelming scent of his aftershave. My legs felt suddenly weak.

Like a child discarding a present it had proudly bought for a parent, but now realised was worthless to an adult, I tried to empty from my mind everything that I had planned to say to Alex. That wasn't difficult: those thoughts were all too prepared to escape from my consciousness anyway — like facts crammed into the mind for an exam, they were meaningless and useless by themselves, with no reason for existence. But my grief was more difficult to ignore, especially after Alex phoned in sick at nine-thirty, just as I had begun to hope that he was simply going to be late.

I went through the remainder of the day in a dour cloud, calculating the probabilities of all the various reasons Alex could have for being off that day. Was he genuinely ill? Did he regret sending the birthday card and hope that I would have forgotten it by the time he returned? Was this his way of getting revenge on me for not letting him know about my Monday holiday? By the time I was on my way home on the bus, I had decided that such speculation was a waste of time and energy: time would eventually give me the answer to my questions. No sooner had I decided this than I looked out of the bus window and noticed that it was raining: was it raining where Alex was? What was he doing at that precise moment — watching the rain, cosy and snug with his wife? Was today their anniversary — did he return to champagne in bed with her after he had phoned in sick?

On the second day of his absence a sick note arrived: he would be off for the rest of the week. On the third day, Ann and I went to the *Black Stallion* at lunchtime.

In the weeks before that, I had managed to free my relationship with Ann of any romantic overtones. Since I was male, she female, and we were both isolated from the other members of staff by a common bond (our youth), we were expected to have *some* sort of special relationship beyond being just workmates, so we became brother and sister — not the real-life, jealous, spiteful, one-upmanship version, but the storybook ideal: Peter and Patricia Pan. We allowed ourselves to become innocents in the eyes of our cynical, jaded elders. Ironically I only managed to persuade the others that there was no passion in our relationship by a display of affection towards Ann, realising that the others had mistaken my previous reserve for shyness, shyness for emotional involvement. Only when I began to take the initiative with Ann — offering to help her out if I had free time, praising a new hair-do — did the rest of the staff sense that I was not in awe of her as they had supposed, and the rumours stopped. Now I was risking the possibility of starting up rumours again by inviting Ann out to the pub.

But I was more than willing to jeopardize the platonic sheen of our relationship. Apart from the fact that I had come to depend on the Friday lunchtime drink, I wanted to release some of the tension I felt over Alex. Whether or not Ann and I actually discussed him or not was neither here nor there. What mattered was that I should be allowed to bathe in melancholy and anxiety naked, unrestricted by the stoical armour I had worn for the past three days. I wanted to spend an hour in an atmosphere of drunken gloom, from which I could emerge refreshed and optimistic. The topics of conversation were unimportant. I knew Ann's repertoire by heart: there was nothing in it which did not lend itself to being cast in a sorrowful light.

When we arrived at the *Black Stallion*, I sat in Alex's seat, Ann in mine. 'Who would have thought, when we were little dreaming boys and girls, that we would end up bank clerks.' I prompted Ann, who already exhibited signs of nostalgic tipsiness after only one Cointreau and orange: a true friend. As she meandered once more along that path which had brought her to this town, this job, this pub, this seat (a path lashed by rain, speckled with unforeseen pitfalls, I reminded her), I relived time spent in the pub with Alex.

I was trying to see things from his angle — literally as well as metaphorically: noting where the light created shadows on Ann's face, and how far she had to turn before her gaze was concealed. I eventually tired of Ann's story, as I knew I would do when I became drunk. She was still exhibiting the same dreary picture she had painted for me months ago: a cluttered room, precariously tidy, like a row of tin cans, eager to fall into chaos at the first sign of carelessness; Ann in the foreground washing, cleaning, sweeping, cooking — her face white, overall black; in the background a rocking chair, a sick old woman seated in it, one eye closed, grateful, content, the other staring widely at Ann; just visible in the distance through the window, the battered little stone above her father's grave, surrounded by plastic flowers and weeds.

I began to talk around Alex, hoping that the scent would be recognized and followed: wasn't Mary furious when she discovered that he was going to be off for the rest of the week? 'Don't think she has ever cursed so much in her life. Probably isn't even ill . . .'

'It's a great laugh, him and Mary,' Ann said. 'They're like Laurel and Hardy. The place has been a lot brighter since he arrived.'

'I think he likes you,' I told her, hoping that she might reveal a little of what (if anything) Alex said to her when I wasn't there.

'So I gather,' she replied, and I realised instantly, like a decorator with crumbling plaster in his hands, that I should never have attempted to peel off this particular layer.

'What do you mean?' I asked abruptly, as though she had insulted me.

'Roy told me.'

'When? What did he say?'

'He simply informed me that I had "another admirer",' Ann replied, letting her head bob up and down like one of those toy dogs you see in car windows: this was in imitation of Roy's absurd mannerism.

'It means nothing,' she shrugged. 'I was in the safe filing; Roy came in, saw that I was trapped on my own, and used Alex as an excuse to leer over me for five minutes. He was probably hoping that I would put Alex down or something: you know how jealous he is of him.'

'Well, what *do* you think of Alex,' I said quickly, before Ann had a chance to question her tone of defensiveness.

'I told you,' she said impatiently, 'he's a good laugh. He brightens the place up a bit.'

'Physically.' I must have said this too loudly, because the barmaid, after a judicious three seconds, turned around slowly to watch us.

'Quite good-looking.'

'Only quite!' Ann looked at her watch, her half-finished drink, my anxious expression, and smiled, the way actresses in old films do, when they realise that they are in a position of power.

'Well, obviously he's terrifically well built — but his clothes are so old-fashioned and shapeless, and he's so big and clumsy: I hate that stupid awkward way he moves about to compensate for his height — he doesn't have to keep showing off how tall he is — we can all see that.' She finished off her drink and placed the empty glass in front of mine.

'But I — I've heard a lot of the girls say that they like that.' I picked up our empty glasses and headed for the bar. 'Aren't women supposed to like big, muscular men?' I asked innocently.

'This one doesn't!' she shouted over. The barmaid gave me a suspicious look as she poured the drinks.

'Why are you so interested in what I think of Alex anyway?' Ann said when I returned from the bar. For one

64

glorious moment I thought that she knew, that at last I had someone I could discuss Alex with who knew both of us. Then I looked again at her eyes, her smile, and realised that she simply thought that I was jealous, fearful that she might prefer Alex to me.

'Oh, I was just hoping for a bit of scandal in the office,' I said unconvincingly. 'He is married, don't forget.' I began to steer the conversation back to familiar territory, embarrassed at my hypocrisy: I encouraged Ann to tell me about the father who had died when she was so young. That was a more comfortable topic of conversation to listen to as I tried to fit this new piece into the jigsaw puzzle of Alex's character: now both Ann and I were forming fictional personalities from dubious interpretations of biased observations, using as instruments unreliable emotions. Ann was perplexed by the change in direction of the conversation, but too drunk by then to work out the reason.

We returned to the bank with time to spare. Ann was giggly and loud, but I had no difficulty concealing my drunkenness.

I decided to go out that Friday night, instead of waiting until Sunday again — partly because I was less worried about bus timetables, more confident, after the previous week, in my ability to win a boy and a bed for the night, but mostly because I was too desperate to experience such a situation again to wait until Sunday. I found the contemplation of another night of sex the only thing that would keep Alex out of my mind for any length of time: fantasies about these two preoccupations constantly traded places in my mind as I dressed and bathed to go out. The dreams I indulged in, though, were less precise than they had ever been. I found it impossible to imagine the future in any great detail, now that real human beings were involved in it. I could no longer plan ahead a week or even a day, so such long-range fantasies as what would an affair with Alex be like — or Pat — or what would it be like living with another man, were completely unimaginable.

I didn't tell my parents until the last minute that I was going into town. When my father noticed that I was ironing new jeans and taking so long in the bathroom, he questioned me through the door about my plans for that night. When he expressed uncertainty about my 'wandering the streets of Glasgow every weekend' I reminded him that none of us had ever been attacked or mugged in all the years we spent in the East End, that I was nineteen, and that other boys my age were living abroad by themselves. In the end, though, I had to pretend again that I was staying at Maurice's. I felt that they accepted this excuse too, as though they were searching more for an alibi for themselves, should something go wrong, rather than satisfaction that I was going to be safe and well.

The Vintners was packed out to the door when I arrived. Again I was driven back against the wall, drink held out a foot in front of me in order to escape the splashes that the jostling crowd was causing. I looked carefully around the room, even going so far as to stare at couples embracing on the seats in the far away corners — but there was no Pat. His absence made me feel lonely in a way that I never had before: my mother and father were always there, so I never had the opportunity to miss them; it never bothered me on the odd day when Maurice was off school sick: and Alex's absence was, by then, almost a relief. When I wasn't with him, a part of me was calm, neutral, empty: like the bank accounts between business hours, there was no prospect of amendment to our relationship. I could not say at that time I yearned unequivocally for his company in the way that I did for Pat's. It struck me that things were liable to become complicated if I were to form such strong emotional attachments with every man I thought I had a chance with. I smiled when I remembered my previously rigid moralizing, and the black and white judgements I showered mercilessly on characters in films and TV shows. I know I smiled because someone came over to me and asked why I was smiling.

I was slightly startled, in the way that I had been startled by Pat the previous week (although this time the curtains opened onto a sun dimmed by a film of clouds). I began to worry about the tendency I was acquiring to lapse into deep introversion whenever alone and drunk: for one thing it made me too easy a target for undesirables. The man alarmed me again by the contemptuous look he drew me when I didn't respond to his question quickly enough.

'Oh, it's okay — don't bother,' he said, as I began to speak. 'I know the type: I'm forty-two and you're twenty-one and can get anyone you want so why should you bother wasting your time being polite to me.'

Did I really look twenty-one? I made a mental note to conduct a survey among the people I knew.

'You've got it all wrong,' I said, grabbing hold of his jumper — which was Brilliant White, a colour I had until then refused to believe existed outside soap powder or paint commercials. 'I was just lost in thought: I didn't even see you until you began to walk away.' This was not strictly accurate, but I didn't want to make enemies unnecessarily after only two visits to the pub. The man looked warily at me, obviously unconvinced. I had never before been so aware of the amount of expression that could be revealed in the eyes: nobody had ever turned such scorn on me before.

'Young people can be very cruel,' he said. This was not exactly news to someone just out of high school, but I listened intently to his complaint, trying hard not to seem too much like a 'young person' — whatever he thought that was. I knew what an old person was, but I found it difficult to visualize his conception of a young one: was it someone more self-confident than he was? Someone who wasn't attracted to him? As he spoke, I was watching my reflection in the mirror behind him, rehearsing various moods with my eyes. I was astonished to discover how difficult it was to control the signal that the eyes gave out — almost as impossible as checking the flow of blood to the cheeks when embarrassed.

The man I was talking to — Vincent — was like too many of the men in *The Vintners*, too clean, well groomed and perfumed. I preferred the ones who looked as though they had just wandered in off the street on a whim: their untidy clumsiness was far more attractive than Vincent's meticulous sterility. This sterility extended to his mental capacity too. Whenever I attempted to argue with him, calmly and methodically, on behalf of my age group, he cut off every argument with a curt one-word reply or a brusque rebuttal, delivered with the aggressive certainty of a spokesman for a militant pressure group. It soon became obvious that he could not live with a good opinion of anyone younger than himself and maintain his self-esteem at the same time.

'But if you were my age,' I said finally, 'and could "get anyone", would you go home with yourself in preference to everyone else here tonight?'

There was no snappy rejoinder to that, an argument which clearly had never occurred to him before.

'Well, I would speak to me at least,' he said indignantly. All the time I had been speaking to Vincent, he had been punctuating his sentences with one hundred and eighty degree turns, gazing over the customers as he did so. His nervousness reminded me of Pat, sitting next to me on the sofa the week before, too shy to force me to devote my full attention to him. But whereas Pat collapsed into my arms at the first sign of encouragement, realising deep down that I wanted him, I felt certain that Vincent was too certain of his unacceptability to do anything other than shatter like brittle ice under a pick-axe at any sign of involvement from me or anyone else.

As I expected, he left during the first short lull in the conversation, obviously afraid that I would soon become bored and humiliate him by making up some flimsy excuse to get away.

'Well, I don't want to cramp your style,' he said, squeezing through the crowd towards the bar. I would, in fact, have preferred him to have stayed. I had already decided that I was out of luck in the pub that night — unless another little Pat popped up out of nowhere. Like the week before, all the better-looking customers were either sitting down in the corner seats, locked in ecstatic embraces, or part of some crowd, whose happiness and exuberance intimidated me.

I slipped out of the pub half an hour before closing time. There was a quarter moon in the sky, a cosmic quotation mark, with a counterpart perhaps in some far away galaxy. The snow, which had been a smooth white sheet over Woodhaven that morning, and a powder blue blanket when I arrived in Glasgow, now resembled the dirty brown stuffing from the inside of a mattress, windswept in mountainous heaps by the gutter.

The disco was darker than the pub: this fact thrilled me, like a sexual innuendo on an invitation card. The music was the same unfamiliar throb from the pub, only this time the building was almost empty and the noise was that of a wild animal trying to get in not out. Although there were only half a dozen people in the hall — spaced out symmetrically, as though someone had placed them all there at the same time — I had an overwhelming impression that I was being watched by a thousand eyes. I couldn't help investing every move I made with theatrical overtones: when I ordered a drink, I did so self-consciously — eyebrows arched, wide smile, turn, sip — every movement exaggerated, as in a TV commercial. The feeling that I was an actor walking on to a stage increased as I went hunting for a space, and the lights scaled the rainbow, pausing at violet when I stopped at a seat, then launching into a different sequence altogether, with a different record, as I sat down. I chose not to sit in one of the luxurious-looking seats to my right, which were grouped together in communal squares, calculating that I would become too isolated when it became busy; and I decided not to linger by the bar or the long, bare wall in front of the dance floor because I thought that this would make me look pathetically over-eager. I finally settled for a space between chairs and wall, which gave me the widest view of the rectangular hall. Now all I had to do was wait.

He was older than I liked: that is, he looked and acted older than anyone I had found attractive until then — his actual age I never asked, although he couldn't have been more than early thirties. I also disliked the rigorous interrogation he subjected me to — as though he were interviewing me for a job I had little chance of getting. No attempt was made to moderate the tone of voice or rhythm of the conversation as he spoke: it was simply name, age, address, occupation, hobbies, and then a lascivious appraisal of my face and body. I could sense he was running through a checklist in his mind: face (smooth, young, masculine); height (tall — but makes him too slim looking?); arms (hairy, nice); penis (difficult to tell — certainly no prodigy).

He approached me after I'd been in the disco for over an hour, but he had passed by earlier, allowing me then a ten-second appraisal, which also encompassed the leather-clad man on my left, and the puny blond to my right. Physically he wasn't bad: firm, sun-tanned, tidy dark hair, cleverly dressed in a baggy suit to disguise what his thin neck and waist suggested was an unexceptional physique. What he had, he certainly made the most of. With his down to earth, businessman-like attitude, I was startled to learn that he was an actor. He seemed a bit annoyed that the name Frank Woodward was unfamiliar to me — apparently he made a very good living from adverts, radio and the odd television play: hadn't I seen him on the STV series at eleven-thirty on Sunday nights? He gave me a run-down on all the Scottish actors who were gay — none of the names he mentioned were surprising in the least. Then we made a tentative arrangement to go home together, and he left to go over and meet some friends, an excuse which allowed him to investigate the new faces that had appeared in the time he was speaking to me.

Someone asked me to dance — this one had no chance, but I danced with him anyway out of politeness. While I was twisting and twirling on the dance floor, I was able to get a good look at the crowd in the disco: it was predominantly young, as opposed to the pubs I'd visited until then, although there were a few familiar old faces from there too — including Vincent, surely either the eternal optimist or a glutton for punishment.

I smiled over at Vincent as he passed by my line of vision; the boy I was dancing with smiled foolishly back at me. As we came off the dance floor, I collided with Alex, who was going on to it. We both stared at each other disbelievingly: the shock and confusion that comes from seeing someone you know well in unfamiliar territory left us both speechless for ten seconds.

Alex spoke first: 'Paul! Wait for me. Don't dare go away.'

He was very drunk — drunker than I had ever been able to get him, I noted sourly. I felt confused as to what my attitude should be — although I knew I was annoyed, in the way I had been the day he returned from the pub at lunchtime with John. The instant he began to speak, desire and reserve began their furious race to the surface of my consciousness, with dignity waiting at the finishing line, the comely prize. It was by then a familiar contest: why then did it always come as such a shock to me when it occurred?

Alex was dancing with a very young, very camp boy, who wore a look of amused toleration (surely the 'young' that Vincent had in mind). I stood at the side of the dance floor for a few minutes watching them. Alex was a terrible dancer — the worst on the floor. His tall, powerful physique was made for lifting sacks of coal or building walls, not for dancing — unless it was pogoing with a pneumatic drill. His legs stretched twice as wide on the floor as his partners, and his elbows were constantly jabbing into the person behind him. His size and his drunkenness caused his attempted twirls to separate him from his partner and get him in the way of other dancers. Every time he re-established contact with the blond (who seemed happier by himself, half-dancing, half-posing in front of the mirrors), he clutched at him tightly — partly to indulge in a romantic embrace, but mostly to prevent himself from falling over. Every now and then I caught him glancing into the crowd, perhaps trying to seek me out. I slipped away back to my space at the wall: he would find me if he was interested enough in doing so.

By the time Alex did find me I had been rejoined by Frank, who was doing his best to convince me that every gay actor he had ever met was a talentless moron. Although his bitter vindictiveness irritated me, I was grateful for the distracting chatter — there was too much to think about by then, and I was too drunk to come to any useful conclusions on my thoughts anyway. It was beginning to become obvious how little I could take for granted: when it seemed as though Alex was taking a special interest in me — and especially after I received the birthday card — I had begun to hope that he would turn out to be a frustrated homosexual, longing for escape from his marriage, and that the only thing keeping us apart was his wife. Now I could see just how naïve that hope was: it was madness to assume that just because one aspect of my fantasy seemed to be coming true, against all the odds, every other aspect would too.

Alex handed me a drink when he finally found me. 'I saw you from over there,' he told me, communicating one of those unnecessary pieces of information that drunkards think it vital to impart. He totally ignored Frank, who stayed nevertheless: I was obviously number one on his list at that moment. Alex leaned his right arm on my shoulder, a pose I had often seen him adopt with the other boys in the bank. It was a pose I found erotic, but when he first began to assume it I was disheartened because it seemed such a characteristically heterosexual gesture.

'Get any birthday cards this year?' he whispered to my ear, the smell of the booze overpowering the aftershave scent.

'Hundreds,' I replied. 'Had any illnesses lately?'

'Me? I'm as fit as a fiddle.' He flexed the bicep of the arm which was resting on my shoulder, and the veins brushed against my cheek like wet sticks of liquorice. For once his apparel did his body justice: light blue jeans, and black T-shirt, clinging wet, so that it followed the three-humped ripple of his torso — abdomen, diaphragm and chest — as he breathed in and out. He would have been completely overwhelming had his face not been so contorted with drunkenness.

'You shouldn't drink like that,' I said, the words trickling out of my mouth as uncontrollably as an incontinent's urine.

'I don't usually,' he replied, straightening up. 'I've seen the effect it has on other people.'

'Well, some men can handle their drink and some can't,' I said, wishing that every conversation didn't have to end up in a battle of wits. But we seemed to have gotten into a situation which was impossible to get out of without one of us overpowering the other: like two tightrope walkers who had begun to walk towards each other we were both travelling on journeys which could not be completed until one of us crashed to the net below — or retreated.

'I love you,' was all I wanted to say, I realised now, with Alex leaning against me — contorted face or not, terrible dancer or not — but we had created a situation in which

72

that was impossible. The only thing I could hope for was some sort of miracle which would allow us both to cross each other in mid-air, then saunter off towards the end together.

I wanted to ask Alex why he had been off all week, but that concern would have given him more power over me, I would be pushed farther back into the corner. So I began to ramble on about what a good week it had been at work — not too busy, not too quiet — what great laughs I'd had at lunchtime with Ann. Alex began to listen with the same unnerving concentration he had used to make Roy look so ridiculous when he was boasting: I became totally insecure about what I was saying, as when an unruly audience suddenly hushes and the speaker fears that what he is spouting is unworthy of such dedicated scrutiny, resulting in his babbling on about the first thing that comes into his head, exaggerating like mad — as I was doing, hoping that Alex would stop staring intently at me, ear cocked, waiting for the point of my speech. I ended my glorification of that horrendous last week in a mumble, turning suddenly as though I had recognized someone across the hall.

'And to think all this time I believed everybody hated the bank as much as I did,' Alex said sarcastically. 'You make it sound so good that I can't wait to get back on Monday.'

Frank had gone to the bar while I was speaking to Alex. He drifted back over but sailed past when he noticed the tone of our conversation.

'Are you with that monster?' Alex asked me.

'I just met him tonight: he's an actor too.'

'As well as who?' Alex said: his eyes were flashing, and he suddenly didn't seem drunk anymore. I had spoken quite seriously and innocently, but I realised instantly that I had hit some sort of nerve, and smiled, as though the remark had been intentionally derogatory.

'I'm not an actor, Paul,' Alex said, in control again. 'Maybe one day: right now I'm a bank clerk.' He smiled, 'Just like you.'

Alex and I had been moving out from the wall as we spoke, so that I now felt rather isolated in the middle of the hall; most of the others had spread themselves out along the wall like a roll of wallpaper.

'I'm just dying to meet Mrs Anderson,' I said to Alex, peering into the crowd, my hand shielding my eyes, as though I were gazing into the sea. 'Where can she be hiding?'

'Friday is her night off,' Alex said calmly, obviously having expected the question. 'Weightlifting, I think.'

'She's not a lesbian, is she?' I asked stupidly.

'Oh God, no.' Alex seemed embarrassed: I sensed a barrier go up — which made me all the more determined to tear it down. He wasn't going to humour me in the way that I humoured Ann.

'What pubs do you usually go to?' Alex asked suddenly, before I had a chance to ask more about his wife. I told him where I had been that night. He said that he was there too.

'I was downstairs.'

'Oh, that's for prostitutes and old men.'

'Well, I got somebody alright last week,' I said; but he didn't seem to be the least bit concerned about that.

'I'm staying with friends in Glasgow if you haven't any-where else to go,' Alex said, studying his watch.

'I think this guy expects me,' I said, nodding over towards Frank, who was still hovering around. If Alex's invitation was simply a room for the night and no more, then I knew I would have felt like a whore in the morning — whether we ended up sleeping together or not. I also didn't want to run the risk of having to listen to him revelling in another room with the blond boy or anyone else. If he did want to sleep with me, then I didn't want it to be under those conditions: I wanted it to be arranged and special, rather than just something that occurred by default, by accident, just because I happened to be there.

I was hoping that Alex would suggest something for later that weekend, but when Frank returned he simply said, 'See you in the shoe box then' — one of our nicknames for the bank — and drifted off into the crowd. Frank, thinking that 'The Shoebox' was the name of a pub, informed me, with an air of mutual congratulation, that he too had somebody 'lined up' for the beginning of the week.

74

Sex with Frank was unsurprisingly clumsy and unerotic. After a few minutes of exploratory kissing and rubbing he produced, from under the bed, a tube of lubricant and two condoms. Having checked and rechecked the fitting of the rubber I allowed him slowly — slowly! — to enter. As soon as he was two inches in I pushed him back out again — it felt as though I were being split in two. He smiled (nothing serious — a miscalculation), handed the tube to me, and lay stomach down, bum in the air. I was surprised by how easy it was to get inside, and how good it was to feel friction all over, but just as I was beginning to enjoy the rhythm and forget my inhibitions, Frank climaxed with a shudder.

'All that for that,' he said, throwing a dirty towel over my head: I withdrew, too self-conscious now to continue. When he was in the bathroom I masturbated, visualizing Pat's denim shoulders and Alex's sweaty black torso.

When I awoke a few hours later, Frank was still sound asleep, facing the wall — the same position he had adopted when he jumped into bed, apologizing for cold feet. I slipped out of the flat before he awoke, leaving half of the taxi fare, which he had paid when we left the disco. It was eleven thirty: I decided to pop into *The Waterloo* on the way home, determined to make the break from Woodhaven last as long as possible. It was an exhilarating novelty for me to make a short journey from one part of the city to another, after the lengthy treks I'd had to endure in and out of the countryside. I could almost fool myself into believing that I actually stayed in Glasgow again.

I felt so much more master of my own destiny, rejoicing in even the most mundane options available to me — such as whether to take a bus or a tube from Byres Road to the city centre.

At the pub I got into a conversation with a couple who were sitting at the table Maurice and I used to sit at in the days when I thought that one bar-fight and a biased evaluation in a magazine meant a pub was eternally damned. That phase seemed so long ago by then. I had learned to decode the prejudiced judgements of middle-class entertainment raters and recognized that 'Rough' was actually Friendly, and 'Trendy' not.

I thought at first that the boy who was with the older man was the one that Alex had been dancing with the night before, but when I got closer I realised that it wasn't: this one was even younger and more effeminate. The older man introduced himself as Robert, but the boy gave no indication that he was aware of my presence as I sat down beside him, even after I rocked the table, spilling his fruit juice and forming a small orange puddle, which crept back and forth towards the edge of the table whenever one of us leaned on it.

'This is Frances,' Robert said, gazing fondly at the boy, who was tall, skinny and blond. The way he sat, long legs bent into the shape of a rhombus, hands in his lap, motionless save for an intermittent sip at his drink, made him look like a puppet, most of whose strings have been cut. Robert seemed content to let the boy sit throughout our conversation in silence, only referring to him after he had disappeared into the toilet.

'Frances isn't really into meeting strangers today,' Robert told me. 'He's going through a bit of an anti-people phase at the moment and can only handle one-to-one relationships right now.'

Frances told me precisely the opposite story when Robert was at the bar, claiming that Robert was too dependent on him, and that he wanted more company.

While I was busily attempting to relate Robert and Frances's behaviour to my relationship with Alex, I suddenly felt a cold hand on my neck.

It was Pat.

'I didn't realise you came here.'

'Otherwise what?' I said, pulling up a seat for him.

'Otherwise I would have been here every day looking for you,' he said, and I blushed.

'I've just popped in from work — at the off-licence next door.' He was talking too loudly and gesticulating wildly, the way he had done the first time I met him. He handed a bottle of dry Martini to the barmaid, who winked and slipped it onto a shelf. I smiled when he came back from the bar and said to Robert, 'Something shady going on there I think.' Robert, who had been staring lewdly at Pat from the moment he walked into the pub, was only too eager to share the joke, bursting into rapturous laughter. Frances was staring sullenly at the orange juice puddle, trying to tip it over onto Robert's lap.

'I was only returning a carry-out I got in here last night,' Pat said; his baby cheeks were pink. He nodded towards the door: 'I'm not supposed to be here — I'd better get back.'

We left together, and I walked him all four yards to the shop he worked in. The loneliness I felt when I turned to head for the bus station was overwhelming, but I had Pat's phone number at last, and I promised to arrange some meeting soon.

On the bus home, I drew the passengers' hostile looks and resolved to find a place to stay in Glasgow immediately.

Consummation

The wedding of Maurice's sister in May turned out to be far more of an ordeal than I had anticipated. What seemed like one of the longest days of my life began with a pious Protestant wedding service, throughout which I had to listen to the minister (who, it was rumoured, was a valium addict) preaching like an evangelist about the love of a man for a woman being akin to the love of God for man. For half an hour he lectured us about the virtues of chastity and monogamy, alternatively attempting to blackmail the congregation into godliness by the use of dire threats about the fate in store for the fallen, or worse, trying to lure us away from sin by the evocation of an extremely vaguely described heavenly paradise. The sermon, unfortunately for him, was not having anything like the effect he desired: we could all see the backs of the bridesmaids at the altar, quaking with helpless laughter.

'In God's eyes,' the preacher warned, in a bellow which would have been more appropriate coming from one of the shifty-eyed con-men at the Barrows selling cut-price curtain material, 'there is only *one* woman for every man he creates, and one man for every woman.' One of the bridesmaids let out a snort of laughter at this, followed by a series of fake sneezes, presumably attempting to disguise the nature of her outburst, but in fact, only serving to draw more attention to herself.

I began to feel as though the devout sermon was aimed directly at me, the greatest sinner in the church (and Catholic too), so I made a point of acting as out of synch with the proceedings as possible — not bothering to open the hymnbook, leaning back on the seat behind when I should have been standing, and letting my gaze wander around the chapel as the minister spoke. But these tactics only left me feeling petty and unrevenged by the end of the service.

Before the coaches could drive the wedding guests to the reception, we had to endure a long, boring wait while the wedding photos were taken. The only good thing about this event was that it gave me the chance to eye up Maurice's attractive cousins and neighbours, who looked as uneasy and odd in their wedding suits and ties as I thought they would. The poor photographer had probably never faced such an intimidating collection of scars, blunt faces and hostile grins. I found it stimulating to watch how sensually they moved to accommodate their discomfort with the unfamiliar clothes: they were constantly flexing shoulders inside bulky jackets, pulling up razor-creased trousers that were too long, or checking zips and rearranging penises in those that were too tight. I imagined them moving with the same embarrassed self-appraisal in the shop when the clothes were bought. They seemed to find it necessary to ridicule their friends' and their own smartness, ostentatiously straightening each other's ties and sniffing suspiciously at any sign of aftershave.

'Oh, get away from him — he's wearing Musk!'

'It wiz ma ma that boat it!'

Two fifteen-year-old brothers with kilts on were constantly exposing themselves or each other to every passing female, their father alternately scolding them and chastising their mother for making them wear the kilts in the first place.

The photographer seemed to have worked out on a calculator every possible permutation and combination of photo-

graphs that could be taken of Maurice's family and friends.
It was only when the rain appeared, fifty minutes into the
session, that we were allowed to board the coaches and
head for the reception. During the meal, the older men
sat rigid, petrified by the castigations of their wives, who
lectured them constantly — warning them not to spill food,
ordering them what to eat, what not to say and where to
sit. The men tolerated this behaviour patiently. They knew
that when the meal was finished, the tables pushed back and
the bar opened, that they could let loose: it would be their
territory then.

The meal was a nightmare for Maurice. His father and
mother — who loathed each other — were sitting only
two seats away from each other at the table. He had tried
to have them seated further apart, but that was impossible,
given that the bride's family all had to sit at the same table.

'I kept hoping up to the last minute one of them would
catch cold or break a leg or something before the wedding,'
Maurice told me.

Even from where I was sitting, two tables away, I could
hear Mrs Burns snarling, 'Whit's that bastard sayin' noo?'
every time her husband opened his mouth.

Finally, after the last dessert spoon had been taken from
the slowest eater, we were let loose at the bar. I determined
to settle down in a corner, get as drunk as possible and think
about Alex. But I found it impossible to get even moderately
inebriated, the drink having been very obviously watered
down. The music was just as weak: pop standards murdered
by a local amateur group — but I danced to one or two
anyway, simply to relieve the boredom, and to get closer to
some of the hunky boys on the dance floor. I even managed
to talk and joke with some of them, no longer so intimidated
by their masculinity — a confidence I had developed from
observing Alex's easy manner with other guys.

I had been sitting chatting to some of the girls from
Maurice's classes at St James, who he had invited to the
wedding, but when I returned from the bar I found that
Maurice had separated my seat from the girls' by two and
a half feet — the precise social distance which divided
the other parties in the hall. Maurice was possessive of

his newfound friendship with his classmates in the same desperate, guilty way that someone who finds money on the street is possessive of it.

I ignored my previous seat and rejoined the company.

'Who's that boy sitting there on a table all by himself?' I asked Maurice. I was bored with the girls' chatter and wanted to demonstrate my growing boldness with the types of guys who had overawed Maurice and I at school.

'It's my cousin, Jamie,' Maurice replied suspiciously.

'Why don't we go over and talk to him,' I said. 'He looks awfully lonely.'

'Aye, go on,' one of the girls said. 'He's been sitting there himself all night, poor boy.' I stood up and marched over with my drink and Maurice's, before he had the chance to argue.

''Kin hardly move efter that meal,' Jamie said when we reached him, clearly self-conscious about the forlorn image he was putting over. I had guessed from his shy manner earlier in the evening that he considered himself too unattractive to compete with the more self-confident guys who were hovering around the available girls. I would have loved to have been able to communicate to him in some way what utter nonsense this was: he was one of the best-looking guys there. He had the sturdy, well-proportioned sexiness that only shortish, slightly overweight guys (like Pat) have. But he probably felt inferior to the tall, lanky boys at the bar, whose scrawny physiques and spindly legs were so unattractive, if only he knew it. Jamie had a handsome face, but one which was cratered with severe acne. To my mind, this only added to his overall cuteness, but to him, it was probably a cross he had to bear in life.

'What do you think of the music?' I asked him, placing my pint between my thighs on the table, like he had done. Maurice was standing by my side, casting longing glances over at his friends.

'Dire,' Jamie replied. 'Even worse than at my brother's wedding. Were you at that?' I shook my head. 'Morry was there, weren't you?' He glanced past me towards Maurice. 'Talent wasn't as good though,' he added wistfully, as a blonde temptress passed by. 'Some fuckin' stoaters here

81

tonight!' His eyes were wide with lust, sad with bitterness. He made no attempt to conceal the hopelessness from his voice, obviously labelling Maurice and me as fellow non-starters.

'You can say that again,' I said, staring at the hard jaw, with its attractive layer of stubble — a half-growth intended to hide the acne no doubt.

Maurice took a step backwards, appalled by my brazenness; but Jamie was oblivious to me, his eyes darting from one girl to another on the dance floor.

'Why have you been sitting here all night?' I asked, sliding off the table. 'You should be up there at the bar with the others.'

'I suppose you're right,' he said, staring at the pint between his legs. 'But I'm too drunk now. I made a right fool of myself last year — and I'm not going to repeat the mistake this year.'

I picked up my drink. 'Well, if you don't join the race you can't lose, I suppose.' I dared to slap him on the back, turning to Maurice. 'But as I've said to Morry many a time — you can't win either.'

I felt really evil that night. I couldn't settle down at all and wandered from table to table, listening to the crowd I had joined gossiping about the one I had just left.

'Promise me you'll never vote Tory,' Mrs Burns said to me as she passed by, holding my neck with both hands.

'Cross my heart and hope to die,' I said, freeing myself from her vice-like grip.

Mrs Burns and her crowd were taking up more space and making more noise than the rest of the guests put together. The more well-to-do members of the clan — the ones who, like my family, had graduated from the East End to the better-kept schemes — were contemptuous of the Burns Mob, who were by then all ecstatically and uninhibitedly drunk. Every now and then delegations from the well-to-do, Carntyne crowd were sent over to chat to Mr Burns, sad-eyed teetotaller and honorary member of their clique. When I moved among Mr Burns' crowd they were denouncing Mr Burns ('Fuckin' Gentleman Jim') as being too stuck up to dance, preferring to play out his favourite pose — the martyr with his orange squash and tomato juice. There were whispers about his strange personality and capacity for quiet cruelty.

'You don't have to scream and shout to be a bastard,' one woman summed up succinctly. I listened carefully and greedily to their talk. I had been listening recently to as much gossip as I could about other people's relationships, searching for some magical convergence of experience which would give me a solution to my problem: what to do about Alex. This relating of other people's experiences to my relationship with Alex was a bad habit I had fallen into during the past four weeks that we had been sleeping together.

The Monday after the disco, Alex had little to say about our meeting, limiting his remarks to banalities such as 'How's your head today?' or 'I thought you'd still be sleeping it off.' This was exactly the sort of behaviour I had been expecting. It conformed exactly to the pattern which was developing in my relations with Alex: some incident would occur which would, to my mind, draw the two of us closer together — Moira's telling me that Alex had been concerned about my absence; the birthday card — but there would be no follow-up to the episode. Time would pass, and I would begin to suspect that I had actually imagined the incident. Such significant events seemed to be occurring more and more frequently, events which I believed would change my situation decisively, but which instead only seemed to make me more anxious and discontented, eager for more progress.

I had the eerie feeling with Alex that everything we had done and were going to do together had been planned out from first meeting to last: it was as though we were simply following a script we were powerless to alter, the plot of which I was incapable of speeding up, no matter how much I wanted to. I knew by then that it was a mistake to expect one simple solution to a mass of different problems, but I couldn't help believing that peace of mind would come only when Alex and I sat down together and had a Big Talk about how we felt about each other. Although I felt that this was the logical answer, in his company I was hypnotized, unable to exert my will over the script which, for all I knew, was written by him.

I realised by then how conceited it was of me to have believed that I would be the first man in Alex's life. I should have listened to Vincent, who warned me on that Friday night that my ego, presently a healthy, virginal white, would be unrecognisable in ten years' time, when it would have darkened and withered, like the body, from exposure to hostile elements; invisible now, he said, it would become all too visible, like a sick relative, when it began to age and die.

After Friday night, I had to consider the possibility that Alex had played the scenes he was playing with me — or similar ones — dozens of times before, with dozens of different actors. What I had to be on the look-out for now was the fluffed line, the mistimed exit, the slipping out of character: I needed evidence that this drama (comedy? tragedy?) was different from all the others, capable of freer interpretation and improvisation.

I resolved not to be taken by surprise by the next incident, to make more of it than I had of the others. It wasn't long before I had the chance to test my resolve. On Wednesday, Alex informed the others, 'Paul and I are going for a long drink today.' This I heard as I came back from closing the outside doors at eleven a.m. It was the monthly half-day in the bank. I remembered that we had spoken of having a drink in the *Black Stallion* on a day that we didn't have to go back to work, but there had been no firm date set. I wondered if the idea had occurred to Alex a second before he said it, or had he not mentioned it until the last minute, knowing that I would comply, in order to exert the maximum amount of power over me? I began to suspect that every little thing he did, every raised eyebrow, had been shrewdly calculated to have the maximum impact on me.

It was becoming obvious I would have to resign myself to the fact that I was going to have less and less control over the important events in my life than I would have liked. I felt sure that if Alex and I had arranged to go to the pub that day it would never have happened — every other time I had planned something significant (the meeting with Jim, the

84

confrontation with Alex about the birthday card) it never occurred.

Now here we were in the *Black Stallion* again: familiar set, if only I knew which character I was to play this time. We had enjoyed a long, slow breakfast in the café across the road from the bank, and arrived at the pub at twelve thirty-five — the usual time — as planned. But, perhaps predictably, our enjoyment of the following hour was not enhanced, as we had hoped, by the lack of a time limit. As the normal time to leave approached, we tried to trick our minds into believing that the drinking had to stop at one twenty-five — but when the time came, there was no sense of relief, simply apprehensiveness at the prospect of so much freedom. Alex and I regarded each other with the mutual embarrassment of two people beginning to realise that they have been conned by the same trickster.

'Even Jake's in a funny mood today,' Alex said, referring to the stream of asinine novelty records that a crowd from the insurance office had programmed to hog the jukebox. After two, when the pub almost emptied, the atmosphere became even more depressing: I began to worry that the afternoon was going to end up like one of those aimless school holidays, when the precious time was frittered away too quickly.

'Is that the middle of April already?' the manageress of the pub said to us, remembering that the bank half-days occurred every third Wednesday of the month. 'God, it'll soon be Christmas.' She had been wiping our table down, but eventually ended up sitting with us, listing her worries and woes in the same drab monotone that she listed the pub's requirements to the man from the brewery. I didn't mind her company though: at that point in my life she was one of my favourite people in the world. To her there was no Paul Robinson or Mr and Mrs Anderson — there was simply Paul and Alex from the bank. She seemed to regard the idea of Alex having a wife as unimportant and irrelevant to the *Black Stallion* universe as I did. She knew from our first conversation that Alex was married, but never ever referred to the fact. That day she delighted me by asking where *we* were headed after the pub.

'Glasgow,' Alex replied, like a magician producing a rabbit from a hat.

I was glad when we left the pub that the sky was pleasantly grey: the only brightness that seemed appropriate to drunkenness was warm coloured neon or candle light. It was strange travelling into Glasgow on the bus with Alex, pointing out landmarks that were almost invisible to me, having passed them so many times. I felt as proud and awkward as a child leading its mother around the classroom for the first time.

We had planned to do a tour of all the gay pubs in Glasgow (all five of them) but in fact stayed in the first one we arrived at — upstairs at *The Vintners* — captivated by the music, which was an energizing mixture of sixties and seventies favourites.

'Poor old Jake hasn't got a look in,' Alex said, pointing to the source of the music: a huge reel-to-reel tape recorder. 'This one doesn't even have to stop to catch its breath between songs.'

It seemed to me, as Alex and I listened and drank, that I understood perfectly the emotion and message in every lyric and chord change; that those songs, when they were written, were intended only to be listened to under the influence of drink. The minister at Maurice's sister's wedding was wrong: surely God had created music for alcohol and alcohol for music — surely that was the divine union akin to his love for man. Alex and I, sitting side by side in a corner seat, ooing and aahing at Spector and Motown, watched the waves of drinkers come and go: the early afternoon crowd stayed to mingle with the five to six, after work one-pinters, then drifted home with them, leaving a quiet pause before the evening customers began to trickle in after seven.

Often there was a wave from the crowd, which Alex returned; sometimes an exaggerated stare, which he ignored. Nobody approached us, thank God, although I was grateful and proud of any recognition of Alex and me as a pair — even if it was only an illusion, even if it was only as the singer sang, *Just For One Day*. This was enough for now: the music, the drink, being seen with Alex, being with Alex, Alex and Paul, Alex.

'When was the first time you had sex with a boy?' I was brave enough to ask him, with a full pint of lager on the table to help if I couldn't cope with the answer.

'Fifteen — then a few other guys. Then Diane.'

'Do you find girls sexually attractive?' Sip.

'Not so much now. I did then though, Christ.'

'Did you really like Diane then?' Gulp.

'Oh aye. Sex every day — sometimes twice. It's amazing how she never got pregnant.'

'Did you love her?' Gulp. Gulp. Gulp.

'Oh aye.' Alex stopped drinking and gazed at his finger, which was circling the top of his glass, perhaps seeing Diane and himself in the circle. She was a totally formless image to me. I had managed to avoid seeing the photos he had passed around in the tearoom on his first day, and I had never heard him describe her. Any description would have meant little to me anyway. I was glad my rival was female: males I could hypothesise into gods on the basis of a one-word description.

'Oh, the Walker Brothers!' I shouted, in an attempt to snap Alex out of his reflective mood. But when he registered recognition of the record with an even more vacant smile a depressing thought occurred to me: some of those records must have associations with his wife — but which ones, and how would I be able to tell?

I must then have slipped into a reverie of my own, because I wasn't aware of Alex putting his arm around me. I only became aware of its presence as I tensed up to nip off to the toilet. When I felt it there — Alex's right arm on my left shoulder — I submitted to it only a fraction of a second slower than Pat had submitted to my own embrace. When we kissed, finally, I kept my eyes shut tight — not so much to hide my own feelings from Alex, but to shield his from me. It was enough, anyway, to run my hands though the river of black hair, to let our brows glide over each other, and to trace the sweat on the back of his neck. I had no idea how wet we both were until we touched; no idea how far apart we had been, or how intimately two bodies could be shared. In the toilet I decided that nothing was going to prevent me from sleeping with Alex that day.

We left the pub at seven thirty and travelled to one of Alex's friend's house — which required us to get off the underground one stop after Frank's, I noted, with the absurd sense of trivia that alcohol sharpens. Although there was a large living room and bedroom and the place was empty, Alex led me into a small spare room, which was stuffy and smelly. I looked at the bed, which was unmade, embarrassed at the thought of Alex and other partners on it.

'Sorry about the mess,' Alex murmured, switching on the small bar heater and positioning it next to me. It was eight o'clock. It suddenly occurred to me that my parents would be watching *This Is Your Life* and worrying about me. But they slipped from my mind when Alex began to undress.

'You look like Clyde,' I told him. 'You know — Bonny and Clyde.' He was still wearing the black shirt and white tie that he had turned up for work with that morning — the clothing regulations being somewhat relaxed on the half-day holidays — and that permanent cool, dark shadow on his cheeks and neck and above the upper lip that I always found so erotic (it was like a continuous, sinful reassertion of masculinity) had by then sprouted into a prickly growth of rough black hairs.

He stopped undressing, dangled a pen from his mouth like a cigarette, and struck up a gangster pose, thumbs hinged in pockets.

'What else do I look like?' He slipped off the tie, unbuttoned the shirt, and leaned against the wall, staring vacantly into the distance.

'An unemployed layabout?' He shook his head, went over to the window and opened it wide. 'Here's a clue: six a.m. on a winter's morning: the sun is just beginning to light up a strip on the horizon. I'm in the middle of nowhere — can't you smell the fresh country air? You are a bright light in the distance, getting closer, closer . . .'

'A hitch-hiker!' I went over to the window, stroked the stubble on his chin. 'Want a lift?'

Despite the fact that I had been drinking for several hours, I was immediately hard when I finally saw Alex naked for the first time. As I had expected, he looked so much more compact without his clothes on. He was hard too, his penis pointing at the light bulb, which he dimmed from a switch on the wire until it was a modest circle.

Alex was clumsy. At first he was on top of me — his muscles redefining themselves with every thrust, like a figure on film going in and out of focus — but he was so heavy that his exertions almost suffocated me and I shifted off to the side. Then there was the by now familiar testing game: rubbing, sucking, wanking — but this time it seemed to go on forever. Currents of sweat were pulsing along the outline of Alex's muscles, despite the draughts of cold air from the open window. Alex seemed as unsure as I was about the next move. Although both as hard as iron, the alcohol in our system was making it frustratingly difficult to achieve orgasm. I began to worry that Alex was going to associate me with drab, difficult sex — but he saved the day by making a joke of the whole situation.

'Right you bastard!' he shouted at his prick, grabbing it firmly and rubbing it vigorously until it admitted defeat and yielded up a few milky white spurts.

Alex was asleep within seconds. As soon as I realised that he was sleeping I felt suddenly wide awake and sober. I looked at him as he slept with the awe and fear with which parents must look at their newly born children. To experience such a miracle with the five senses didn't seem to be enough. I could see the figure, unequivocally handsome with its bright red cheek on the pillow, lips parted like a baby; I could hear his sighs, touch his hardness, taste his salty sweat, and smell his sex — but it wasn't enough. I felt a vague dissatisfaction with this being which had radiated itself into my consciousness — a dissatisfaction akin to that nagging anxiousness I had felt as I approached puberty and my body began to react to all the sex around it which it had managed to ignore for so many years. I could only hope that I would discover a mechanism, as I had done then, which would allow me to relieve the tension. What that mechanism would be, I had no idea — but I was sure by then it wouldn't be anything as mundane as sex.

I felt that what I needed was some sort of emotional orgasm: I wanted to find out everything there was to know about Alex, from the day he was born until that moment, in one blinding flash: then I would be able to take Alex apart bit by bit, to discover the essence of his being and the reason why I loved him. But even if I could label all the components of the emotion — sexual attaction, personality, unattainability — would I be any less in love?

I drifted off to sleep for two hours. When I awoke, Alex was still sleeping, although now his face was buried in the pillow, his body stretched out full length with his feet sticking out comically from beneath the sheets at the bottom of the bed, spotlighted by the circle of light from the bulb. I was sober by then, but when I looked at Alex, I saw him with the eyes of a drunkard — as I had always done, I realised then. Every detail of his body was unusually fascinating and particularised: if I touched his hair, it seemed like no other hair on earth; the chain around his neck seemed to be lying at the only angle possible out of all the angles in the universe.

From a room next door came the sound of a television set being switched on. The news was just finishing. I jumped out of bed and ran to the phone, a towel wrapped around me modestly. I explained to my mother that I had decided to stay overnight at Maurice's 'after all', feigning surprise at her emotional reaction to the sound of my voice: hadn't I told her that I was meeting Maurice in Glasgow after work?

'We were just about to phone the police,' she yelled at me. 'Your father has already been down to the bank to see if there was a break-in or something.' I could hear his shouting in the background. When he came on the line I hung up, pretending that we had been cut off.

When I awoke the next morning, Alex was up and dressed. He had shaved off the rough stubble, but the sinful black shadows were there, as always. I felt that potent randiness that comes along the morning after a night's heavy drinking. Unlike the night before, I could have climaxed within five seconds if Alex had shown any inclination for a quickie before work. He didn't — although there was no sign of regret or embarrassment about what had happened in his manner.

'Here's to you, Mrs Robinson,' he sang as he placed a tray of tea and toast in front of me, and we traded smiles which were intimate and competitive at the same time. I wondered if he was affectionately playing with my name, or simply remembering the boy who had waved over the night before when the song was played. Later I decided that it didn't matter: from now on it was Our Song.

When we left the dingy flat the day seemed to rush up madly to greet us, like guests at a surprise party. It had obviously just stopped raining: half the people in the street still had umbrellas or hoods up. There was a crazy kind of clarity to the day which made me feel that I was seeing through a newly polished window that I hadn't even realised was dirty before. The rain on buildings, faces, clothes, concentrated colours and sharpened contours, so that every image seemed intensified and vibrant — as though that old woman with the poodle, wearing the yellow, glimmering mac, was every middle-class old lady trying to cross the road. The streets were dark silver, and their wetness revealed little nooks and crannies unusually invisible; only the sky was a dull slab of concrete grey — but the dimness of the light helped sharpen the already distinct outlines of the people, buildings and cars, the mesmerising quality of the day completed by the shimmering reflection in the puddles on the ground, adding depth and chaos to the scene.

It was a joy just to walk down the road with Alex, to stop and look in a shop window, to have someone come up to us and ask the time. I felt I could at last understand all those couples I had laughed at as they tripped over themselves in the street, wrapped around each other, supposedly indifferent to their surroundings, but actually as self-consciously together as two actors on a stage.

Alex and I weren't late for work as I had hoped, but we were so early that by the time the others arrived we were in the tearoom enjoying a second breakfast. Nobody actually asked us why were were doing this, preferring to gossip among themselves when they congregated outside the tearoom.

'Aye, that's right — they said they were going to the pub after work.'

'They look as if they've been here all night!'

I was in high spirits for the rest of the day.

'I don't know what you two were up to on your day off,' Rose said when she caught me singing in the safe. 'But can I come next time too?'

The staff's indirect enquiries allowed us to be suggestively evasive about our activities until eventually Moira, who had no sense of gossip, asked us outright. We told her that we had been to a party at one of Alex's friend's house, and stayed the night in Glasgow.

'Don't you let that Alex lead you astray,' Moira said, turning towards him. 'He was such a nice quiet boy until you started working here.'

The day of Maurice's sister's wedding had been dull and overcast; the day after, the sun was splitting the trees. By the time I arrived at *The Vintners*, the air was still warm and the sky bright, although the sun was so low that several streets, completely covered by huge, dark shadows, were as damp and black as a coal cellar.

'Don't worry, he's only popped into the toilet,' Ronny, one of Alex's friends from the drama society, told me when he noticed my anxious glance towards the space where Alex usually stood in the pub. I was relieved, having convinced myself that I could hardly expect Alex to be there after I had deserted him the night before for the wedding. But then — and this, in the end, was the reason I had finally decided to attend the wedding — Alex could hardly complain if he was left without my company every now and then, since we had yet to make any firm arrangements to meet at the weekend.

Although we had met every Friday since the first day we slept together, I disliked the informality of the routine — Alex simply asking me every Friday on the way out of the bank if I would be 'in town' that night. Presumably, since there was no stated commitment, we could both have gone our separate ways every week — but we invariably ended the evening by slinking off into our corner after socialising for a while with Alex's friends.

Jim and Walter were sitting at one of the tables in the middle of the pub. I gave them a frosty nod, as I had done

92

ever since the first time we met in the pub and Jim had apologized for not keeping our date at St James all those centuries ago. I would have liked to have chatted with them about the history of their relationship and to gossip about St James, but pride, and the sullen, doomed atmosphere they radiated (the affair was plainly nearing an end) prevented me from doing so.

'I thought this was my lucky night!' I replied to Ronny, wondering if there was just a trace of jealousy in his sarcastic greeting. Ronny was forty-eight, five feet two, and grossly overweight, but I suspected even the most unattractive of Alex's friends of being a former 'affair' — a term I thought seemed curiously pessimistic the first time I heard it, but which began to appear more realistic the more I saw and heard about the fragility of many gay relationships. When I was with Alex and his friends I was constantly on the look-out for any signs of former intimacy, alert, whenever I returned from the toilet or the bar, for indications that attitudes or topics of conversation were being subtly altered with my reappearance.

'Yes, apparently half the Citz' crowd was there,' Alex said to Ronny when he came back, returning to a conversation he had been conducting with him before he went away. I was granted a surly nod of recognition, as though I were a former customer who had returned to the pub after a long absence. Then I was ignored: that was to be my punishment.

'But then anything by Tennessee Williams . . .' Ronny said. I was sitting in Alex's seat; Ronny was at my right and Alex was standing to his right. I could tell by Ronny's uncomfortable position in his seat — body facing left, head turned away from me to face Alex — that he was embarrassed to be ignoring me, but he was hypnotized by Alex's eyes, which stared defiantly away from me.

The situation pleased me in that it indicated that I did have some power to affect Alex. Also, the longer he ignored me, the more likely it would be that the night would end with the sort of confrontation that I had dreamed of, allowing us both to be open about our feelings for each other. But no sooner had this occurred to me than Alex went over to the bar, returned with a pint for me, which he placed in my hand, and asked me how the wedding went, as though I had just appeared in the pub that instant. The timing of the ending of Alex's mood with my decision that the situation was beneficial to me was so precisely coincident, and I so mesmerised by Alex, that I began to wonder if he was capable of telepathy.

I reported that the wedding reception was great fun, but the ceremony itself was a bore, mentioning the laughing bridesmaids. I was determined to sound as dispassionate as possible and showed no annoyance with his initially cool reception; nor did I reveal my disappointment that an opportunity for confrontation had been missed.

Alex and I stayed longer than usual that night socialising in his corner. As had happened every other week, a swarm of friends and admirers congregated around Alex. The ones he introduced me to seemed dull. They were mostly fellow amateur actors, obsessed with the trivia of a drama underworld I had no idea existed in the city. Unlike Alex, who had often enthused about some project he had worked on, they did little to transmit their passion to me. Until that night I had assumed that my low opinion of Alex's friends was due to the fact that I only ever spoke to them at the beginning of the evening when the conversation in the pub was tentative and lightweight; but as the hours passed, voices were raised and inhibitions lowered — and I was no more impressed with what they had to say. I felt sure there must be something to them I was missing — why else would Alex have them as friends?

Half an hour before closing time, Alex and I pushed our way into a newly vacated seat in a corner. When we got drunk, Alex became much more passionate than me: I was always inhibited by the people around us and the far away, but still perceptible, glances of his friends. I could never become as involved in the passion as Alex could — after that first time together, when our kisses became routine, and it was obvious that our intimacy was not going to change anything as I had hoped. I also felt that the onlookers knew, as they stared or glanced at us, that they were watching a magnificent sham: to my mind, although by then Alex and I spent as much time together, and went through the same motions, as two people in love, there was always something missing: our life together was like a beautifully photographed, perfectly scripted film which was ever so slightly out of focus — so slightly that it took an act of will to perceive the imperfections: Alex's wife, questions unanswered, declarations still to be made.

When we awoke late the following morning, the sun was shining magnificently behind the thin curtains in the spare room in the West End that we had continued to use — a room unaltered since the first night we spent in it: I dared not tempt fate by attempting to create some sort of nest for Alex and me.

Why don't we go somewhere? Why don't we do something different, rather than spending all weekend in the pubs? I wanted to say, as the scent of fresh, dewy leaves wafted in from the open window, and I listened to the sounds of early summer — boys playing in the street, families heading for the seaside — passing us by. But at the same time as I desired some sort of confrontation about the way things were going between us, I was also scared to risk upsetting the precarious equilibrium of our relationship at that stage: having got that far, I felt it best to let Alex decide when to alter the momentum of our little journey together. Life had become almost pleasurably simple now that I had been forced to relinquish all control over my own destiny: my function now was simply to wait and react to the Next Thing that happened.

We were both sitting up in bed with glasses of Irn Bru resting on our stomachs, willing hangovers away so that we could have something to eat and go out to the pub again. My glass of the rust-coloured liquid was sunk half an inch into the beer belly I was developing; Alex's rested on a solid line of muscle.

'You drink just as much as I do,' I said to him, clutching at my glass, which threatened to topple over as I spoke, 'yet look at the difference between us.' Alex adopted a sympathetic version of his monkey face.

'That's because I exercise,' he said matter-of-factly. Alex was no narcissist: whenever he did draw attention to his appearance, it was done with the same self-mocking manner with which he flexed his bicep that first night I met him at the disco.

I put both our drinks away and turned on my side, rubbing the remaining wetness into Alex's stomach. 'When?' I asked.

'When I'm not with you.'

'With Diane?'

'Sometimes.'

I let my hand fall away: like all mistresses, I preferred to assume that my lover stopped enjoying himself the instant he left my side. It was the first time since we had begun sleeping together that Diane was mentioned. There were so many questions about her that I wanted to ask — does she know that you sleep with me, does she sleep with other people too, what does she do all weekend when you're with me, does she know about me, how do you describe me to her? But I knew from my reactions to the couple of times he had spoken of her that I wasn't yet capable of listening to the answers.

'Well, then, how do I get into exercising?' I asked Alex as I slid out of bed, dressing quickly and self-consciously, aware that he was appraising my physique.

'Why don't you come out to the gym with me today and find out,' he said, springing out of bed and adopting various ridiculous gymnastic postures.

And of course I did.

I had often wondered what Alex's routine was when he wasn't with me, but I never dared ask, lest I should discover some detail of his life with Diane. I was amazed (and a little hurt) to find out that he attended the tiny sports complex in Rosehill twice a week after work and on Sunday.

'Why didn't you tell anyone at work?' I asked him. I was thinking of how close we had been all those lonely February and March nights when I had supposed he was in Glasgow.

'I didn't want to let anyone know in case Roy or one of the others began to tag along,' he said. 'I don't like to speak when I'm exercising.'

'Well, why are you allowing me to "tag along"?' I asked, thinking that I could trick him into saying something unambiguously positive about me for the first time.

96

'Because I know that you'll keep quiet if I tell you to.' I wasn't sure if I liked that or not, but I forgave the insult (if it was such) when he suddenly clasped his hands behind my neck and kissed me lightly on the lips (his were warm and mine were cold after a swig at the Irn Bru). This was as gratifying as it was unexpected: Alex was usually dispassionate when sober almost to the point of frigidity.

We had to pass through the swimming pool in the sports complex to get to the gym. There were embarrassing shouts of recognition from some of the boys who came into the bank: we were invited to witness their dives and underwater handstands. Seeing the boys so gloriously uninhibited in their own territory, it was difficult to believe that they were the same people who shyly and clumsily slipped in and out of the bank with their little deposit account books, and pay-ins for their bosses.

'I used to dream about seeing these guys in their underwear!' I said to Alex as he dragged me the last few yards to the gym. 'I'll die if the butcher's assistant is here!'

My first impression of the gym was that it conformed to my idea of what a torture chamber must look like — which it must have been to some of the overweight, middle-aged men who used it. The various unhygienic and menacing-looking rubber and metal devices that sprouted from the wall gave off an evil, musty odour — like that of ancient volumes in second-hand bookshops; this foul smell took half the session to become accustomed to. When manipulated, the instruments seemed to bully the user into exertions beyond his capabilities, as though the springs and wheels were issuing a challenge, a challenge bravely answered and then repeated with every heaving grunt and every screaming creak of the appliances throughout the session.

I never spoke a word to Alex throughout the forty-five minutes we were in the gym — partly because I didn't want to annoy him, but also because I didn't want to disturb the atmosphere of concentration that was so intimidating in the small room. Whenever anyone did speak, it was with the same hesitant, guilty whisper that is spoken in church. I followed Alex around the room, attempting to do something, as he did, with every piece of equipment.

Alex paid no attention to me as he worked his way through his own programme, oblivious to anything but the scorecard in his mind. All his tugging, pulling and bending contorted his face into shapes and expressions I had never seen it in before. I wondered if that tight scowl was a caricature of his physical manifestation of worry; or if the busy hand wiped away tears of exertion in the same way that it wiped away tears of grief or joy. As I watched him it occurred to me that I had until then only witnessed on his face flickerings of the more mundane emotions: annoyance, boredom, tiredness, amusement. Orgasmic delight, I had to assume, was that red-faced eyes-closed frown of concentration I had managed to catch occasionally: but Alex was so quiet when he came — almost as though he were attempting to hide his climax from me — that often the only manifestation of his orgasm was the white wetness on his hand or mine, or inside me. Alex exuberant I had never seen except when he was drunk. But his features then were too relaxed, his eyes too cloudy for me to make any sense of them. Alex in distress I could not imagine.

He was as economic with his movements as with his emotions. Perhaps it had been here in the gym, as Alex strained muscle against muscle in tight manoeuvres that his body had begun the erotic dialogue with itself which resulted in the compactness and precision of his gestures. Since even such a simple movement as standing up or sitting down caused numerous muscles to flex and relax in his body, the physical and mental satisfaction this produced meant that there was no need to exaggerate any gesture — as shorter, flabbier men would do, to compensate. I relished Alex's precise manoeuvres ('That exaggerated way he moves to compensate for his height' as Ann ironically described it) — the way he would twist from the waist to let someone pass, or arch his neck and shoulders like an ostrich to get through low doorways — but I often wondered what the adolescent Alex was like: was he a running, jumping thing which had been tamed by the gymnasium?

When he had finished working on all the machines Alex looked exhilarated. His face was as red as the skimpy shorts which clung obscenely to the contours of his firm, round bum. Sweat had deepened the red of the flimsy shorts as he bordered the room, but the redness of his face was fading to healthy pink even as he spoke to me and towelled himself dry. When he left, Alex was glowing healthily, his hair oily with honest sweat, but I looked and felt much the same as I had when I went in.

I bumped into Pat again one day at the end of May. I was at the tennis courts in one of the city parks. Alex and I had set aside Wednesdays for tennis after work, but the reaction of the bank staff to my association with sporting activities embarrassed me and I was forced to change plan.

'What's that, Paul?' Beeny had said to me the day I returned from the sports shop in Rosehill brandishing the first item of sports equipment I'd ever bought in my life.

'Well, I'm not sure — I may be wrong,' I said, holding the tightly wrapped parcel in front of me, 'but it's either a giant lollipop or a tennis racquet.'

'Aye, I can see that,' she said impatiently. 'But what are *you* doing with it?'

I told her that Alex was teaching me to play tennis. Roy looked up from his desk for an instant, then looked back down again, frowning indignantly. This was a grave insult to his status as sporting expert in the office.

'After all you said about how ridiculous sport was!' Beeny said. The others were just as surprised. That was the first and last time that I took my tennis racquet into work. From then on, Monday and Wednesday were for swimming and weightlifting, Saturday and Sunday for tennis. By the end of May I was spending all weekend and half the weekdays with Alex. What did his wife make of all this?

The day I met Pat, Alex and I were playing two of his friends — Jack, whose spare room we used every weekend, and whose house we would be returning to that evening for a party, and Bill, a musician Alex had known for years. The match was really only between Alex and Jack — Bill was as hopeless a tennis player as I was — although he had been playing for three years, me for three weeks. Alex and I were winning: it was the final set, four-two. I was serving against Jack with the sun in my eyes, so we had already written off that game. When I noticed Pat outside the railings of the tennis court, I lost all concentration and every ball I hit went into the net. Alex could see that I was looking off the court every time I walked back from the net.

'What are you looking at for God's sake!' he said angrily after we lost my serve to love.

'It's just somebody I know.' I pointed over at Pat, who was with another boy. Pat suddenly saw me for the first time and waved furiously. Then he noticed Alex and turned back to his friend, with the comic swiftness of a character in a situation comedy.

'Could we just finish the match first?' Alex said, as Jack and Bill waited for us. Dare I hope that he was jealous? He returned to the back of the court to receive Bill's serve without a glance in Pat's direction, thrashing his return of serves into the ground and winning the match for us in less than two minutes. I went over to speak to Pat after it was over.

'I thought you weren't speaking to me for some reason,' he said brightly. 'You've walked past me three times in the pub!'

'Oh, I never walk past anyone!' I told him. I still felt guilty that I had never contacted him as I said I would — just before I met Alex. 'I just get so sloshed in the pub these days that I wouldn't recognize my own mother if she walked past me.'

'Oh, can you imagine it!' the boy that Pat was with said, hands clutching his chest. 'If my mother walked in the pub I'd need to be sloshed — otherwise I'd have a heart attack!'

At the other end of the court Alex picked up my sports bag and indicated that he was taking it to the car for me.

'I've seen you with him before, haven't I?' Pat said, watching Alex carry the two heavy bags to the car. I nodded, hoping that he wouldn't inquire as to the state of our relationship: I wouldn't be able to bring myself to say we were lovers.

'Oh well,' Pat said. 'If you're ever in the neighbourhood come and visit me.' He slipped me a piece of paper with an address on it. 'I'm moving soon to a new flat in the West End.' He turned to go. 'And you can bring Superman if you want to.'

I recognized the tone of bitter sarcasm which I fought to keep from my own voice when I became jealous of some old flame that Alex brought into our conversations.

Pat walked away with his friend, his laughter too loud to be genuine. As he turned to speak to the other boy, I could see that he was glancing back to find out whether or not I had waited at the railings to watch him walk away, which I did — until I knew he couldn't see me anymore.

'You're fairly progressing,' Jack said to me on the way to the car, smiling consolingly when he caught me watching Alex joking with a young blond boy as he handed back the tennis balls we'd hired. Jack was so quiet that he often caught me out watching Alex. He had a soft Swedish seriousness about him with his tidy blond moustache and cool, high cheek bones. When he spoke to me, he punctuated every sentence with a pacific, cheerful smile, which seemed to say 'Cheer up; things could be worse.'

Jack's living room looked smaller than it had done on the odd occasions I had peeked in at it as Alex and I passed on the way to the spare room. As I looked in before going to get changed for the party, I could see that there were already a number of guests there; they were being attended to by a red-haired man in a hideous white suit: Jack's lover Ralph. Alex was changing in the spare room: half-dressed, shirt open to the waist, tie hung around his neck, he looked like an actor in a Martini commercial. As I slipped off my tennis shorts and top and got into my party gear, Alex sat back on the bed and watched, saying nothing. I wondered if he was still angry with me after the business with Pat at the tennis court.

'Beautiful,' he said, when I was finally ready. Then he suddenly jumped up from the bed and gave me a tender kiss on the cheek.

'What's all this?' I said sarcastically. 'Passion! Pinch me somebody, quick!'

'You asked for it!' Alex grabbed my left buttock and squeezed it hard, simultaneously dragging me down on to the bed, where he tickled me. 'Alex, no — my new clothes — pe-p-people outside.' When he finally stopped, he put his arm around my shoulder and drew me towards him, holding tight.

'I wish this were just an ordinary night and we didn't have to go out there,' he said sadly, as the doorbell rang yet again. I looked round at him, but his eyes were closed: this Alex was disturbing.

'We'd better get out,' he said, sitting up on the bed. He turned towards me. 'Look at you, you slut!' He pointed at my crotch and the erection which was visible through the thin white trousers. 'You can't go out like that!'

'Well, it's not going to go away until you get dressed,' I said, stroking the smooth torso, from chest to stomach. 'You're one to talk anyway.' I put my hand on his own plainly perceptible bulge. Alex finished dressing and we both sat up on the bed, arms folded, giggling as we tried to will away the defiant erections.

'Try to visualize big Mary and Moira having it off,' Alex suggested. That would probably have done the trick if he hadn't kept leaning over and giving me long lingering kisses every time it looked as though the swelling was going down.

I had already decided to be bored at the party and pretended to Alex's friends that their talk of art and politics held no interest for me. Some of them became quite aggressive when I betrayed my lack of interest in their preoccupations ('How can anyone not have *any* interest in art? You mean you're happy being a Philistine?') The more anyone attempted to get me interested in his conversation, the more I was determined to play the rigid simpleton: what I was really trying to do was to show Alex up — his punishment for leaving me to fend for myself for most of the time.

Eventually I withdrew into a corner beside Billy, who looked as out of place as I felt. Jack came over and sat beside us as soon as he saw us sitting together. Perhaps fearing that any banding together of dissidents would get out of hand and spoil the party, he sent Billy over to a couple in the far corner who, he said, shared his hobby — astronomy.

'He looks quite happy tonight, doesn't he?' Jack said when we were alone, nodding towards Alex, who was blabbing away merrily with a group of old friends from his year at university.

'Isn't he always?' I said curtly. I resented the fact that Jack seemed to believe that all I wanted to talk to him about was Alex — especially since it was true. Nevertheless I stayed in the corner and chatted with him for some time, becoming irritated as the party progressed and Alex became more and more animated as he reminisced with his friends.

The extremely potent punch circulating the room acted as a depressant on some — I could feel myself sinking into a stubborn sulk — and as a stimulant to others — Jack and Ralph had begun to argue with each other in vicious whispers. I drifted over to the drinks table where Alex — who had gone outside with Billy and his friends to gaze at some constellations — had been chatting with his university friends.

I was only half-listening to his friends' conversation as I poured myself some more punch — until I realised that they were discussing Diane and Alex. There were two couples: the women seemed intent on criticising Diane, while the men were more interested in running Alex's character down.

'*I'm* not surprised it lasted at all,' one of the women said. 'He's just perfect for her — all she ever wanted was some great beauty to show off whenever she went out.'

'—which, unfortunately for poor Alex, was about once a month — if she could bear to tear herself away from her precious books,' the other woman said.

'Exactly: that's why she didn't give a damn what Alex got up to when —'

'—but surely she realises that things will have to be different now.'

What was she talking about? AIDS?

'He's still got that terrible insecurity about being working class,' one of the men said.

'Yes, did you notice that too,' the other man agreed. 'When you said —'

He stopped talking when he noticed his wife's horrified recognition of me standing behind him.

'You're a friend of Alex's, aren't you?' the woman said. 'Don't think we're being nasty about him: we're really all very fond of him.' The husband stepped back as I moved into their circle. 'Yes,' he said, embarrassed. 'We're not saying anything we wouldn't say to his face.'

'I must say I've never thought of Alex as insecure,' I said indignantly. 'One of the things I like best about him is that he seems so confident and self-sufficient.'

The other man there snorted at that. 'Alex is insecure about everything.' The others looked reprovingly at him — but he was obviously too drunk to be cautious. 'Alex is insecure about his background, his accent, his failure at university — that's why he became so infatuated with Diane: he had to conquer the brainiest girl in his year. It's the simple, bare-faced psychology of any romantic love affair — whether it's love of beauty or brains or power: if you can't match it destroy it.' This was greeted by howls of protest from the others.

'That's just too cynical for me,' one of the women said.

'No, that's absolutely true,' the other man said. 'I don't think he's at the destruction state yet —' the first man gave a look that made it plain he wasn't so convinced about that '— but he's obviously trying to match her achievements in some way: Alex dropped out of uni' because he couldn't cope with the work. Diane got a PhD and she's now researching all over the place. All this weight-training and amateur dramatics is Alex's only way of proving to himself that he's something special too — which is pretty difficult when you're a boring bank clerk.'

'Well, some of us have got to do it,' I said indignantly. The man's face reddened when he remembered that Alex and I worked in the same office.

'There must be something interesting about him if he's got you lot still discussing him half an hour after he left you,' I said as I walked away from the two couples. I pointed out the window. 'I doubt very much whether he's talking about any of you out there.'

Despite my defence of him, I was infuriated at the reminder of how small an area of Alex's life he had allowed me access to. When I told him later about what his friends had been saying about him he was not at all pleased — but he refused to confirm or deny any of their theories, making it obvious that there were some things he was simply unwilling to discuss with me. I felt that I was on the tightrope again: everything would be fine between Alex and me if I moved forward carefully, face-forward at all times, never looking to either side of the narrow path laid out before me. But I was tired of that.

'How long can this go on for?' I asked Alex as we undressed in the spare room that night.

'How long can what go on?' he said, yawning.

'This — you and me, you and Diane.'

'That's up to you.'

'It's up to you, too.' I was infuriated that he was taking it all so calmly.

'But I'm not the one that's complaining — you are: I'm happy the way things are.'

'But what about the future?'

'I don't plan ahead like that.'

'But I want a plan. I need some kind of security.'

'There isn't any security in relationships.' He began to shake his head. 'You've only had one relationship — you've got a lot to learn yet.'

I slapped him across the face. He slapped me back, twice as hard. I had hit him out of sheer frustration — we both seemed to be speaking different languages — but I was happy when he hit me back: there wasn't anything more to say at that point.

We spent a restless night together — which is the only way two people trying to keep as far apart from each other in the same bed can spend it. In the morning we both awoke aching from the strain of trying to keep from falling towards the middle of the bed. When I was in the bathroom shaving, Alex snuck up behind me, grabbed me round the waist and buried his face in my neck. I pretended that I was startled, but I had smelled his aftershave the instant he had tiptoed in the door.

'Oh,' I said dispassionately, feigning disappointment, 'I thought you were someone else.'

'I thought you were, too,' Alex said. The way his voice dropped at the end of this indicated that he realised it was not the wisest remark to have made under the circumstances. At any rate, he seemed anxious to make up for any ambiguity in what he had said, turning me around to face him, and putting his hands around my neck. He was wearing the big chunky white sweater that reminded me of the man at the fairground who helped me on and off the rides when I was a child: I looked forward to seeing that man every year — he always seemed so capable, the way Alex had done, and the fleecy wool on his jumper always excited me when it brushed against me, the way Alex's sleeves were doing now.

When I put my own arms around Alex's neck I began to sob silently: the label at the back was sticking up — Alex was so clumsy about his appearance — and suddenly I remembered what they had been saying about him last night and he seemed so vulnerable.

'I do care for you,' he whispered when he felt my tears on his cheek.

I felt like an ogre: I was pressurising him unjustly. How could I expect just to barge into his life and take over?

We spent the rest of the day in Jack's car — Alex was supposedly giving me lessons, but I was such a bad learner and he such a bad teacher, that we ended up agreeing that it would be best to settle for a drive around the countryside. We drove into Woodhaven, saying little on the journey there, which made any attempt to distance ourselves from the incidents of that morning and the night before even more difficult than it was already proving to be.

We stopped the car near one of the deserted lakeside districts. I had begun to cheer up by then and made attempts at starting up a conversation, but Alex was becoming more and more withdrawn. He kept wandering off by himself, standing at the edge of the lake, and peering into the distance. He was wearing the white shirt and black tie from the night before and a long grey woollen scarf hung down over a black overcoat now too. I suddenly realised what the sad but resigned profile against the washed-out, watercolour grey sky reminded me of: he looked like a man at a funeral.

By the time I arrived back home it was very late and very dark.

'Been to see Maurice again?' my father asked me as soon as I walked in the door. I nodded.

'That's funny,' he said, 'because Mrs Burns phoned up to see if Maurice was here today, and she says she hasn't seen you for weeks.'

Frustration

It was the middle of July, but colder than it had been since January. I had woken up several times in the middle of the night, startled by the touch of the cold city air. Eventually I capitulated to the cold and got out of bed to close the window: now it would become stuffy and difficult to breathe. But better to suffocate for a few hours than to wake up in the morning with a cough and a sore throat that would stay with me for a week.

Once I noticed that it was as late as six a.m. I found it impossible to get back to sleep, so I switched off the alarm and lay back in bed, watching the sun rising slowly over Glasgow, as it transformed the heavy cobalt-coloured curtains to tissue-blue. When I was up and having breakfast, I amused myself by trying to decipher the graffiti which had been engraved into the furniture by previous tenants.

I watched a lazy arterial sun glow vibrantly against a pale grey sky as I walked from my bedsit in the West End to Buchanan Street bus station. The pace of my walk varied with the intensity of concentration I devoted to my thoughts: from a strident march, when I was deep in thought, oblivious to my surroundings, to a stroll, when I began to surface from my ruminations and pay more heed to where I was, to a slow ramble, when I had managed to convince myself that I had thought through everything that there was to think about my relationship with Alex.

I tried very hard to keep Alex out of my thoughts for as long as possible: whenever something about him did occur to me, I found it impossible to prevent myself reviewing all our dealings with each other from start to finish with this new insight in mind — and I had to be exhaustive in my thinking, otherwise any omissions would nag at me throughout the day. I had promised myself on so many occasions that *this time* would be the last time I would think about our situation, but there always seemed to be some little detail — a word or a look that in retrospect seemed more important than it had at the time — which just had to be mulled over. I was always aware, though, that spending more and more time thinking about my problems with Alex would not solve them — moving to the West End had given me far more time for that, and I was further than ever from a solution.

The move to a bedsit in Glasgow at the beginning of June had nothing to do with my parents, although the argument we had the night they confronted me was an indicator to them and me that it was becoming impossible for us to continue sharing the same space.

'Mrs Burns hasn't seen me for weeks because I haven't stayed at her house for weeks,' I told them. 'I said I'd been to see Maurice, not the whole clan!' I had launched instantly into the indignant tone — which was this time harsher than ever since I knew I was in the wrong.

'Where *do* you stay then?' My father had his arms folded, playing the scene for all it was worth. I was sickened by his eagerness to play the clichéd 'stern-but-concerned' father: this was real life, he would be thinking, just like on TV.

'With various people — people Maurice and I know from school.'

'Why didn't you mention any of these "people" before?' As usual two answers came to mind: the truth — all of it — 'Because if I told you where I really went and what I really did, I would also have to tell you . . .' and the lie — 'Because I didn't see the point in giving detailed descriptions of my every movement and of people you'll never meet anyway.'

'Why will we never meet them? Why don't you invite them back here for a change instead of gallivanting into Glasgow every time you want to meet them?'

'There isn't any point — I'll soon be moving into Glasgow to stay with them — just as soon as we can get a flat together.' I hadn't wanted to reveal my plans until I had actually found a place but there was no other way of diverting attention from my excuses.

As soon as my parents realised that I was serious about leaving home their behaviour towards me changed completely. Throughout the following weeks when I was in and out of Glasgow regularly hunting for flats, they were much less inquisitive about my comings and goings, perhaps hoping that I would eventually forget the idea if they gave me more freedom.

My reasons for wanting to leave home were both psychological and practical. I was trying to prove to myself that I was still master of my own destiny, having lost so much control over events in my life in recent months, but I also hoped that living in Glasgow would bring me into contact with new friends who would help me to break away from Alex — something I had become more and more convinced was the only solution to my unhappiness.

After the arguments at Jack's party, it was beginning to look as though Alex and I were as close as we were ever going to be. He had soon after begun cutting back on the amount of time we spent together: he stopped attending the weekday visits to the Rosehill sports centre, claiming that he wanted to 'rest his muscles'.

'But don't *you* stop going,' he had said. 'That would be the worst thing you could do at this stage.'

I did manage to attend the centre once or twice alone after work, but I found myself so overcome with loneliness that I stopped. Soon after that, we stopped spending the weekend together when the swimming and tennis became 'too busy'. Since then I had been attending another sports centre in Glasgow. Although still lonely, I progressed much faster in my activities without Alex's critical gaze to inhibit me.

As I was waiting at the bus station, I mulled over a comment someone had made to Alex at the weekend about his 'tennis arm', suspecting that he had resumed attendance at the centre in Glasgow without telling me. What he did on a Saturday afternoon — after we parted with cheery waves, like two school friends — was something I would never dare ask him: I was only too grateful that we were still together by that time of the week — more and more frequently we were parting on Friday nights after some insane argument. The previous week had been typical.

We had gotten into the habit of going on to the disco after *The Vintners* — a routine I might have enjoyed in the past as a prolongment of our cosiness in the pub, but now disliked intensely, due to the fact that in recent weeks Alex and I had been spending far less time alone in public. The hours spent at the disco, apart from being an infringement on what little time we had to be intimate, also left us so impotent with alcohol and exhausted with dancing that we had virtually stopped having sex all together.

The trouble began that weekend after we'd been in the disco for about half an hour. I had been perched on a stool at the opposite end of a small table around which Alex and his friends had been standing; I was trying to remember how many pints I'd consumed in the pub when a young red-haired boy came over to me and asked where Alex's drink was. The question confused me: surely Alex's drink would be next to Alex, who was standing at the other side of the table. But when I turned I saw that neither Alex nor the crowd he had been talking to were there.

'Oh, this must be it,' the boy said, grabbing the only drink still left on the table. I watched him return to the quiet end of the disco and hand the sweaty glass to Alex, who was sitting in the square of low leather seats with the group he had been talking to. The red-haired boy was beaming with childish excitement as Alex thanked him: he acted like a child that had just caught its first fish — like I did the day I washed out Alex's cup for the first time.

So this was to be another little change in our routine that I was to adapt to. There was no point in causing a scene about it: every other time something like that had happened, Alex always furnished some plausible excuse for his behaviour — he would simply smile and claim that he presumed that I would follow when I noticed that he had gone. But I had no intention of joining him: I was, in fact, grateful for the opportunity to escape his company, which was becoming more and more of a strain as his interest in me seemed to be diminishing, and he was acting more and more as though I were invisible.

I began to look around the disco — not as I would have liked to have done, with Alex by my side, proud and confident, but nervously, appraising those around me in a way I hadn't done since my first days in the pubs in Glasgow. When I had first begun going out with Alex the occasional interested stare had been flattering icing on the cake: now those looks were all I had — my only hope for future happiness. I found myself gazing at every above-average figure around me, comforting myself with the thought that *he* would be the one I would seek out when it was finally all over.

I wished Pat were there. I had seen him in the pub that night, as I had seen him on previous occasions, glancing over when he thought I wasn't looking; but he never came over to speak, not realising how desperate I was by then for some interesting diversion — which I was certain that he could provide. Pat was like a book that I had opened in the middle, read a page of, and wanted to read from start to finish; Alex was like a book I had read the same chapter of over and over again, frustrated because I knew I would never be able to locate the other chapters.

Alex came over to speak to me when he passed by on the way back from the toilet — it had become obvious after an hour's separation that I wasn't going to join him.

'George Henderson,' he sighed, looking at me rather guiltily as he tried to pretend that nothing unusual had happened that night. 'I haven't seen him for two years!' He was staring over at a tall, gangly blond boy who was sitting in the seat next to his. Alex had recently begun compulsively to point out every boy in the pub and disco with whom he had enjoyed even the briefest of affairs.

'Are you still on lager and lime?' the red-haired boy asked as he came breezing past on his way to the bar. Drinks had been travelling to and from their table all night long. This was possibly the last time that I could automatically assume that I would be included in Alex's round: another little bond broken. It was as though we were travelling back in time, retracing our steps and systematically severing all the little ties we had formed along the way, like children petulantly smashing irreplaceable toys.

'Are you not coming over?' Alex asked me, as he followed the red-head back to his seat. I shook my head, still dazed by the cold-hearted cruelty of his actions.

I remained on my stool for what seemed both an eternity and no time at all until a voice behind me said, 'You've hardly moved from that seat all night long.' Pat!

No: Jack, surprising me with his silent presence as usual.

'I'm just enjoying being drunk, listening to the music,' I said — the first words I had said to Pat, a hundred years ago.

'And watching the dancers,' Jack said. Alex and the red-head were on the floor, dancing as though their lives depended on it. I looked away: this time I really hadn't been aware I was watching Alex.

'Why don't you find someone else?' Jack asked me. 'Why don't *you* make a move instead of waiting for him to push you slowly away.' This was the first time he had spoken directly about my situation with Alex.

'Because I don't want to give Alex the satisfaction,' I said. I was surprised that I found it so easy to articulate the chaos of emotions in my head with such a simple sentence, like a magician capturing a tornado in a milk bottle. 'If he wants to stop seeing me he'll have to come right out and tell me,' I continued. 'I won't give him any excuse to leave.'

'But that sort of tactic never works,' Jack said, with the pained expression of a teacher explaining the same point for the fifth time to a slow pupil.

'I've known Alex for a long time —' he began, then lapsed into silence when he saw the eager hunger for information on my face.

'Oh, let's just dance,' he said. 'A disco's no place for speeches.'

It was the first dance I'd had all night and I enjoyed it enough to stay up on the dance floor for twenty minutes. When I returned to my seat Alex and his crowd had gone. Just as I noticed, with great relief, Alex's jacket, still draped over my seat where he had left it at the beginning of the night, the red-head appeared and swept the jacket off the stool extravagantly, before I had a chance to sit on it. I could scarcely believe my eyes when I saw him meet up with Alex, who continued to head for the door. I leaped up out of my seat before they had the chance to get away.

'What do you think you're doing — leaving without telling me!' I felt as though my temperature had shot up to one hundred and ten as I stood in front of Alex, blocking his path. He took two steps backwards, as though he feared I was going to resort to violence: Alex hated scenes or confrontations.

'I thought you were after Jack,' he said, looking past me at the door, trying to work out the best possible escape route. The sheer obviousness of the lie was an enraging insult to me.

'What fucking rubbish!' I felt my temperature increase again. 'You know I feel nothing for Jack — how dare you insult me by giving me such a lame excuse!' Jack had gone by then, but if he hadn't I would still have been unable to prevent myself from saying what I did. 'You have no right to assume for your own benefit that I want to go home with every guy I dance with.' He had pulled the same trick before: often when Alex saw me smiling and enjoying myself on the dance floor with a friend of his or a stranger, he would begin to look for his umbrella or start rummaging in his pockets for his cloakroom ticket, as a warning to me. Alex had become so used to my complete devotion that anything less than one hundred per cent attention was treated as a punishable offence.

'Should I assume that you want to sleep with him then?' I pointed to the red-head, who had been watching us argue with the wide-eyed concentration of a child watching someone drown.

'But you're less flirty than I am,' Alex said. 'I have to assume that you're more serious about the people you talk to.' The red-head handed him his jacket and they began chatting, gradually turning their backs on me as though I were a tramp in the streets who they hoped would soon go away — which I eventually did, scowling at the faces who had been watching the scene with amusement, as I glided out of the disco.

As usual, after such a nerve-wracking Friday night, I had tried to spend as much time at the weekend as my body would allow at the sports centre: in the pool and at the gym it was easier to let the mind become blank. At home, all I could do was stare at the walls and wait for the bad feeling to go away, as though it were a bothersome cold. I lost interest in anything but sleep and exercise for days after Alex and I had one of our scenes. I would awake the morning after, innocently happy for the first few seconds, until I remembered the night before. The depression I felt was the opposite of the relief I used to experience on waking from a nightmare: now it was waking life that was the nightmare, and sleep the only haven. Even when I found it impossible to get back to sleep I would stay in bed anyway until late afternoon. As a consequence, my sleeping patterns were becoming increasingly erratic — a process I decided to encourage in order to give some element of light and shade to the days at the bank, which were becoming more and more monotonous.

After almost a year in the office, I was still the junior: for the past eleven months I had been following the exact same routine that was established for me in my first few weeks in the bank. Mr Bentley held the opinion that juniors should not be allowed to take up any responsible positions in the office — even for training purposes — until they had been officially promoted. Effectively this meant until a new junior was appointed. Ann had told me that she had been junior for two and a half years, so a change in my status did not seem a likely prospect in the near future.

Now that I had the freedom of my own flat, I began to experiment with different moods at work: staying up all night then going into work exhausted next day, so that the hours passed in a dreamy haze; other days getting up at dawn and exercising at the sports centre before work so that I arrived there bright and alert. But those mental tricks were proving ineffectual against the overpowering routine of the bank. I was settling more and more for an early rise and a lazy stroll to the bus stop, which put me in a peaceful and tranquil mood — at least until teatime, or dinnertime on a quiet day.

As I walked to the bus station every morning, the early morning city smells exhilarated me: bakeries pumped the cosy, warm scent of newly baked bread and steaming sausage rolls into the streets, and newly mopped shop entrances gave off pungent whiffs of strong disinfectant. No matter what sort of mood I was in, the cold, fresh city air invigorated me in a way that the country air in Woodhaven never could: flowers bloomed and trees grew at an imperceptible pace in the country, but in the city, every morning, a clearly visible regeneration took place, far more exciting than the cycle of nature. Everybody seemed important then — as individuals, and as cogs in the great wheel: dreamy shop assistants, waiting behind counters for doors to be opened, noisy cleaners emptying out of schools and churches, efficient road-sweepers and striding postmen, patient old men behind full paper-racks, and razor-sharp young executives, their faces stinging red with strong cologne and the fresh crispness in the air.

This was the time of day when I most yearned to be free of the bank, with its enslaving nine-to-five routine. What I most wanted to do was to return to bed and fall asleep before the city lost its freshness and vitality, before it fully awoke to reveal its afternoon personality — which was dull and bland when the city clouded over with heat and noise, only becoming vibrant again when cool rain fell with the darkness, and glossy streets mirrored neon.

I was always first on the bus to work, so that I could fantasize that it was my own personal taxi, which I graciously allowed others to use. And I always went straight to the back, spending the first few minutes of the journey peering at the sun, which stood out so round, red and flat against the pale sky that you felt you could have reached up and peeled it off. The trip was doubly enjoyable if a young, donkey-jacketed labourer came up to the back and sat opposite me, half-asleep on the way to his first job.

A few days after the incident with Alex I had recovered enough to manage a smile for the pensioners lined up outside the post office as I passed them by.

I hesitated for a moment before giving the special ring on the bank doorbell (two short, one long): I was toying with the idea of giving it one long ring, knowing that it would send the others into a panic — the bank auditors were due at any time. Even more unsettling than an unfamiliar ring was the banging at the door that occurred every now and then: all eyes would turn towards the warning lights behind the tellers' desks, which would inevitably be shining red, like a row of mischievous cats' eyes — the burglar alarm having been set off by mistake, summoning the police to the bank. At such times Alex would shout, 'Mary, it's a raid — hide your snuff! Paul swallow your poppers!' 'Your whit?' Beeny would say. 'Your whit?' It would invariably fall to me to open the door and let the police know that it was a false alarm — a task I was only too eager to carry out, since it was always the youngest, handsomest cadet that was sent round.

Moira was already arguing with the computer terminal that morning when I passed by her, shaking her head slowly at the printout it was producing. John and Rose were keeping the radiator warm when I went into the tearoom to hang up my coat. They had been engaged for a month by then. It seemed amazing to me, and totally unromantic, that they could work with each other for two years before starting an affair together. The others claimed that there were always signs of it but they were probably as surprised as me. The two of them were so inept at being lovers. Perhaps fearing some scepticism about their new-found passion, they attempted to treat us all to manifestations of their love at every possible opportunity — holding hands together every teatime, sitting apart from everyone else on the radiator, loudly whispering sweet clichés in each other's ear: it was acutely embarrassing, like a schoolgirl's vision of a romance. I decided that there were no strong feelings on either side, simply a realisation that it was about time they were both settled down.

At teatime after they left the room, the second shift speculated on their future, now that they were engaged. Beeny had the most up-to-date information as usual: 'John's being moved to the heavy cash next week,' she announced, delighted at our surprise. There was a rule in the bank that close couples — not only those who were married, but also those who were only engaged — could not work in the same office: this was a precautionary measure to prevent fraud. The separation of John and Rose (at present they were side by side in the office, tellers one and two) would be the first step in the severing of the love cord. Eventually John would be transferred to another branch.

I could just imagine Mr Bentley's shock when he was informed of the relationship: there would be at least one 'Good grief': colour would seep into his cheeks, as though he were a mother who had caught her son with porn, then his face would fall into a frown of concentration as he headed for the policy papers.

Beeny, Dot and Doreen — the other three tellers — were arguing about how the shake-up would affect them. They were speaking with the usual tone of resigned weariness that was present at the table every day, summoned up like a ghost from limbo. But there was also something else in the air that day: Beeny was nervously glancing around the table then looking down at her knitting — a sign that she was about to discuss something controversial and was waiting for the best possible moment to do so.

'I wonder when John will be transferred,' she eventually said, her cheeks reddening slightly. 'I mean, you would think they would want him away as soon as possible.'

'Well, it's a fair rule,' Dot said. Her own refusal to lift her eyes from the table indicated that she was in on this — and that someone present in the tearoom was going to be talked about or referred to.

'There's been so many frauds with couples lately.' She and Beeny ran through a list of all the couple-frauds they had heard about. Dot took a sip of her tea and looked over at Beeny: 'And it shouldn't only be married couples that get separated,' she said. 'What's to stop two relations from conspiring with each other — or two good friends.' I kept my nose in the magazine in front of me, pretending that I wasn't listening. Everybody else in the tearoom was looking over at me by then. I felt as though I was in one of those horror films at the end of which the victim suddenly realises that everybody else around him is an alien.

'Yes — and what if two people were going together and nobody knew about it?' Beeny said. 'Or what about two gay people?' Both Dot and Beeny were blushing furiously by then. There was a momentary lack of nerve as Doreen and Dot looked away from me and began to study cracks in the table.

'I thought the auditors would have been here by now,' Doreen said. But Beeny ignored her.

'I mean,' she said quickly, desperate that the moment she'd taken such trouble to engineer shouldn't be allowed to fizzle out without her having forced some sort of confession from me, 'What if Paul and Alex decided to steal something together?'

'What a great idea,' I said, getting up to leave the tearoom early. 'We were just talking about how short of money we were going to be for the honeymoon.' I wasn't angry that they had begun to suspect Alex and me of having a relationship — only at their timing. It was ironic that it was only as our affair began to cool that the staff had plucked up the nerve to comment on it. I had been quite happily making allusions to my closeness to Alex, but none of the others had picked up on them. It was only when so many of the customers commented on the number of times they had seen Alex and me at the sports centre together that the others began to realise how much time we were spending in each other's company.

I popped into the small Catholic church at lunchtime. Rosehill, I was pleased to discover, was predominantly Protestant. Being in the religious minority was one more thing that added to the distance I wanted to keep from the rest of the staff. It was amusing how ignorant the staff were about any other religion than their own. Maurice phoned one day, as a prank, to 'remind Paul that it's All Souls Day today' (at school he was a militant atheist; I, when pressed, would only admit that I was 'probably agnostic'). John Whiteman, who took the call, was puzzled, uncertain if he had picked the message up correctly. 'It's a Catholic thing,' was all I had to say, and he drifted off embarrassed: Catholic Things, like Women's Things, were mystifying and unspeakable.

Despite the fact that the building was nearly empty, the church was warm and welcoming. I remembered, with regret, the comfort and protection I had felt in church as a child, a feeling that had been burned out of me gradually as the church became associated with things I had come to hate: the hypocrites who were religious for forty minutes a week in Woodhaven, Catholic moralist dogma, boring Sundays. For that afternoon though, the church, if not The Church, was a useful haven from Alex and the rest of the staff.

Beeny tried to steer the conversation back towards Alex and me again that afternoon: the two of us were trapped with her, and John and Doreen around a table, counting and separating notes.

'Did you see Marilyn last night on TV?' Beeny said.

'What's he like?' John chimed in.

'He?' Doreen said, confused. 'I thought you were talking about Marilyn Monroe.'

'Have you never seen him?' Beeny said. 'It's a guy with long blond hair who wears make-up and dresses like a woman.'

'At least he's got some muscles,' Alex said mischievously. 'Not like Boy George.'

'That's his pal,' Beeny said to Doreen.

'Bum-chum more like,' John added.

The recent influx of androgynous, gays-related material into the pop world was a great source of mockery to many of the bank staff.

'I think they should all be shot,' Roy shouted over.

'Aye, they'll never beat Helen Shapiro,' Alex said.

'No, really,' Roy said, placing his pen on the desk before him to underline the profundity of his words. 'What sort of image is that to be presenting to young people at such a formative age?'

'But I'm at a formative age,' Alex said, confusing Roy, who refused to believe the rumours about Alex and me. (How could anyone who went to a sports centre three times a week be a fairy?)

Alex had been glancing over at me, trying to involve me in the conversation. I hadn't spoken to him all week — usually I had given in by Tuesday to his teases — but I felt my resolve weaken.

'Oh!' Beeny's buzzard shriek echoed throughout the office. 'My Brian was fuming last night: did you see that group — the Scottish group with the wee skinhead?'

'Bronski Beat?' John said. 'I know —'

'He was singing about kissing some guy on the lips,' Beeny said. 'Brian was just about to kick the telly in.'

'We've met him, haven't we, Paul,' Alex said, staring straight over at me, so that I couldn't ignore the question. I nodded.

'Where?' John said.

'In a pub in Glasgow,' I said. The silence was as complete and deafening as that following a power-cut.

'Speaking of pubs,' Alex said. 'All this talk's making me thirsty.'

Jake was no fun any more: the golden oldies section, which had once dominated the jukebox, had been reduced to ten tunes, too familiar to be enjoyable.

'How's your swimming going?' Alex asked me when we had settled down into our seats.

'It's like when you were trying to teach me to drive,' I said laughing. 'I'm okay so long as nobody gets in my way — but I panic and lose control if someone even looks as though they're going to cross my path.'

'Well, at least you can only kill yourself in a swimming pool,' Alex said, referring to a near-fatal accident we had one day when I was driving.

'And who would care about that?' I said sarcastically. It was difficult to keep the bitterness from my voice for long:

I hated the way our relationship was drifting back to the chummy workmates state; and I was angry with myself for continually making up with Alex, every concession assimilated.

Alex ignored my tone and asked if I was going to Ann's birthday party in two weeks.

'Is that an invitation?' I said.

'I can't make it,' he replied, embarrassed at the question. 'I just thought I'd let you know in case she was too shy to.'

'You're too kind.'

'She asked me to tell you.'

'Why couldn't she ask me herself?'

'Because she doesn't care if I go or not, but she would be upset if you refused her.' He looked me straight in the eye. 'Do you understand?'

'I understand perfectly,' I said. 'Better than you do.'

I hated it when he tried to pair me off with Ann — what a neat solution that would be for him.

'You really like Ann, don't you?' I said.

'She's got a lot of qualities I like,' he replied.

'Like what?'

'Different things in a man and a woman — they wouldn't be any help to you.' I didn't have to look at my reflection in the tinted mirrors to know what sort of signal they were giving out.

'I'm sorry,' Alex said, when he realised how hurt I was. 'It's unforgiveable to make fun of someone's emotions like that.' He turned and rested an elbow on my shoulder. 'But sometimes you're so bloody arrogant!' I stared straight ahead saying nothing. 'You seem to think that I owe you everything you feel able to give up — that everything should follow the little plan you've got into your head.' He began to adopt a pleading tone. 'Why couldn't you just have been happy with what we had — why does everybody always want more?'

'Alex, you're talking the most utter rubbish.' I moved free of his elbow. 'I didn't — okay, you're right — I did want more, but I never pushed for it. All I've ever done is wait and wait and wait for things to get better —.'

'But that's the point,' he said. 'You make it so obvious you're waiting: you don't give me any chance to give of my own accord — you devalue everything I can offer by your anticipation.' He shook his head. 'And then there's all the other complications.' He stood up. 'I won't be pressurised.'

On the way back from the bar he put *Mrs Robinson* on the jukebox. I smiled dutifully when it crackled over the speakers. I tried not to look too anticipatory but I knew that I was still waiting for the Next Thing — although I realised by then that I was just as eager for some sign that Alex and I weren't for each other as I had been for an indication of involvement before.

While I was waiting for this Next Thing to happen I decided it would be best to start preparing for the Worst Thing, by developing some sort of life away from Alex. I began to go out more myself during the week, dragging Maurice along for company. I had managed to convince him to visit some of the city's gay pubs with me after he saw some of the hunky bodies in the porn magazines I left around the flat every time he visited. I suspected that the realisation that all homosexuals did not look like Liberace was his reason for becoming more adventurous — or maybe it just took some people longer than others: I couldn't really have cared less. All I knew was that he kept me from feeling lonely when I was out without Alex.

I had arranged to meet him the day after I made up with Alex. I got off the bus at his house on the way back from work. When I knocked on his door, the dog immediately began barking in the living room. A dirty, sandy-haired fourteen-year-old-looking boy answered the door. He had a football under his arm.

'I'm —' I began to say, but the boy immediately let go of the door and ran back into the house shouting 'Auntie Jeannie, it's Maurice's pal.'

'Well, let him in for fuck's sake!' she shouted as I entered the living room. 'Honestly, they'd get ye fucking hung!' she said when she saw me. The fourteen-year-old went back out, slamming the door behind him. There were two other, younger children in the room, sitting by the fire — a boy and a girl.

The house was in a much worse state than it had been the last time I saw it. Every corner of the room was littered with unwashed clothes, newspapers and broken toys. I sat in one of the armchairs and immediately sank down in the broken seat until my shoulders were peeking out above the arms of it.

'Go and tell Maurice that Paul's here,' Mrs Burns said to the boy, who completely ignored her.

'Go and make Paul some tea,' she said to the girl, who also ignored her.

'I'll do it!' Maurice shouted from the kitchen. Although it was over seventy-five outside, the fire was blazing away as usual. The coal was piled up in the fireplace, threatening to tip over onto the grate, and richly coloured flames — blue, red and green — roared up the chimney like fireworks. The fire was unguarded, and the two children, both in pyjamas, were poking at the glowing coals, attempting to coax rare purple and turquoise-coloured flames from the blaze. Mrs Burns was in her dressing-gown: I wondered whether she had gotten up late or was going to bed early. It was so depressing to see her sitting across from an empty armchair now that Mr Burns had been taken to hospital with his recurrent heart complaint. The nephews and nieces she had imported were little comfort; they were someone else to swear and shout at, but they could not fill the vacuum created when the strength-giving bitterness Mrs Burns depended on from her husband was taken away.

'What do you think of that for a waste of time,' Mrs Burns said, pointing to the manilla envelope containing Maurice's dismal school results (four fails) which sat on top of the fire surround. Curled up from the heat of the fire, it seemed to cringe shamefacedly behind a mass of cheap glass ornaments.

'Not one pass! Not one fucking pass!'

'Do you like dark toast?' Maurice called in from the kitchen in an attempt to drown his mother out.

'As long as it's not too dark!' I shouted back. 'The last slice he gave me I could have written my name with it,' I said conspiratorially to Mrs Burns.

She was watching the children, who were engrossed in their new game: heating the poker in the glowing red caverns under the coal until it was white-hot, then melting holes in newspapers and plastic ornaments. I was melting in the heat too, my face scarlet from the fire, even though I had pushed my chair back as far as the crumpled carpet would allow.

Maurice brought in a heaped-up plate of toasted cheese and a mug of tea for me, which I placed on the carpet, in the white circle that someone else's mug had left. Then he settled down to tell me about the boy next door, who did his muscle-building exercises in the garden every day. I did not gain the same amount of erotic satisfaction as Maurice obviously did, squirming in his seat as he described the pounds of meat and protein the boy's mother complained she had to buy to fuel such a powerhouse. His attitude reminded me of my own not so long ago. Maurice still saw men as abstract, untarnished ideals — he saw only types: dark, blond, hairy, smooth. None of his images had any of the infuriatingly ambiguous traits of real people.

Mrs Burns asked me if I was still working in 'that fucking money shoap'.

'Still there.'

'Yer aff yer bloody heid,' she said, the same comment she made when I told her I wasn't going to stay on at school to get enough Highers to go to university. Mrs Burns saw university, and in particular the grant that went with it, as one other way that the poor could get some of their fair share of the Tory economy.

'It was either that or the Civil Service,' I said. 'Would you rather I was working for Mrs Thatcher then?'

'That bastard! She's the fucking cause of it all!' She pointed accusingly at the television set which was broadcasting a toilet roll commercial: the one with the little dog in it.

'If you've any sense in you,' she said, pointing at me now, 'you'll get your highers, take your grant and fuck 'er!'

Maurice and I got up to go.

'That clock's fast!' Mrs Burns shouted as we left the house.

'God, it's like a sauna in there,' I said to Maurice when we got outside. 'You should charge admission prices.'

'I know, I can't stand it,' he said. 'She builds up that fire all day, then has to stay up half the night to wait for it to go down.'

We met a group of Alex's friends in the pub. They were the only customers there, so it was impossible to avoid them as I usually did.

'No Alex tonight?' Brian said. He was half-sitting on the knee of his boyfriend Richard, who was staring into my eyes, as he always did when we met — whether Brian was with him or not.

'Not often we see you in here without him.' I said nothing.

'Are you not speaking to each other?' Richard asked.

'Of course we're speaking to each other,' I said curtly. 'I see him every day at work.'

'Are you still going out with him?' Brian asked.

'I never was.'

'Oh, come on,' they both said together. They had heard this before.

'It was an optical illusion.'

'You've been in here together every week for the past three months.'

'I was here and Alex was here,' I said wearily, 'but we weren't together: we just happened to be here at the same time.' I knew that they would report everything I said back to Alex. Brian was annoyed: he had probably gone through the same sort of experience I had with Alex, and was damned if he was going to hear it described in those terms.

'I saw him with his wife last week,' Richard said to Brian.

'Oh her,' Brian said, sparking off an argument as to the properties of her personality: Richard, who had been to university with Alex and Diane, claimed that she was extremely intelligent. Brian disagreed.

'Academically-minded — but not intelligent.'

'She was brilliant — God! Alex really trained you well, didn't he?'

Brian banged his glass down on the bench behind him. 'Richard, will you stop talking about something you know nothing about. I've known Alex for years; I went with him for six months. You were hardly more than a one-night stand — and that only because you followed him all over the place at university.'

'What does his wife do when he's not with her?' I asked to shut them up: the bickering was becoming embarrassing now that the place was filling up.

Brian and Richard traded glances of malicious satisfaction.

'Well, they used to go through phases,' Brian said. 'Alex used to be very secretive and untruthful with Diane and she hadn't a clue — until it all came out into the open.' He smiled smugly. 'Until *I* made sure it was all out in the open.'

'Then there were the arguments and "trial separations",' Richard said, 'which lasted until Alex stopped seeing whoever was unlucky enough to be involved with him at the time. The last separation was legal though.'

I began to hope again: 'A divorce?'

'No, just a formal statement — presumably an attempt by Diane to retain some dignity — and shock Alex into better behaviour.'

'Obviously that's what the baby's all about, too,' Brian said.

'They're having a baby?' I said, shell-shocked by all the new information.

'I didn't know that either.'

'Alex only found out himself about a month ago.'

It was only with the sudden clarity that shock can bring that I became aware that Pat was standing next to me. I realised that he had been there for some time, waiting for me to notice him. Maurice had drifted over to chat to some guys in drag who he had been camping it up with the last time we were there. Love seemed to bore him.

I went over to sit at a table with Pat. I couldn't bear to listen to any more talk about Alex.

'I haven't seen you around much, Pat.'

'I've been staying in — saving up for when I move.' I stared straight into those bright, happy eyes — eyes which suggested an innocent, contented nature, incapable of committing a single act of cruelty. As he sat beneath the spotlight above the table, the gleaming white sailor's top he had on shone like snow at the top of a mountain, his yellow crew-cut glittered and sparkled like a halo, and the silky perspiration which glossed his skin vaporized into a thin mist which evaporated in seconds — the way love should do in the face of indifference.

As usual, his excitement was pleasantly infectious. I found myself copying his habit of lifting his glass to his face and lowering it again two or three times before drinking from it.

I asked him where he was moving to.

'I'm getting a council flat in Barrowfield; the West End flat was too expensive.'

'Barrowfield!' It was the Harlem of Glasgow — a derelict housing scheme deserted by all but addicts, alcoholics and the criminals who lived off them.

'I know — but I haven't got anything valuable to steal — and I'll be better off: I'll have three rooms — I can rent out one or two.' He was talking very loudly and quickly and gesticulating. I felt guilty that I had deflated his little dream somewhat.

'You'll be rolling in it,' I said. 'With your money from the off licence, and your landlord's income!'

He lifted his pint with both hands and took a sip. 'So if you know anyone who wants a very cheap room . . .'

When he went over to the bar for a drink for us I began to think about Alex again: was he pushing me away because of Diane's pregnancy or would it have happened eventually anyway? Or was it my 'pressurizing' him that was putting him off?

The pub door opened and another of Alex's friends came in, followed by Alex himself, who began to chat to Pat when he saw him at the bar. Pat pointed over to where I was sitting and Alex came over.

'Do you know Pat?' I asked.

'Once,' he replied smugly. 'A long time ago.'

'This is disgusting,' I said, standing up. 'The whole thing is disgusting.'

'It was long before you met him,' Alex said, sitting down at the table.

'It's not only that — the whole thing is becoming too chaotic.'

'Well, you know what to do if offends your morality.' He was becoming angry again.

'It's not a question of morality. I — I think I love you.'

I had thrown away my shield at last and trusted in the mercy of my adversary. Alex didn't seem startled, but he didn't seem to know what to say.

'You've never made it plain what you feel for me,' I pleaded.

'You know I'm very fond of you,' he said. 'I thought we had discussed all this. I'm not going to run to keep up with someone else's emotional timetable.'

We were speaking different languages again.

'I'm being hurt too much.'

'Why can't you just relax then?' Alex said. 'It's you that's making love into such a painful thing.'

'There's no point in us seeing each other any more,' I said, heading for the door. 'I can't live from one day to the next like this.'

Pat was standing at the bar with a pint in each hand.

'Phone me at the weekend,' he said as I passed out the door.

The next day at work it was obvious that Alex had chosen to take my words at face value: he returned the few odds and ends he had of mine, trying to appear as neutral as possible — neither sad nor relieved — as he did so. I spent the following weekend at home, afraid to go out in case I found him out enjoying himself on his first official night without me.

The next week the auditors turned up at last and we were all kept in late every night — a restriction I was grateful for, since it gave me less time to sit at home feeling sorry for myself. There was little for anyone to do on those nights, but we all had to stay behind anyway. It was an odd sight as we all milled about the office, glancing over furtively at the auditors who were dotted about all over the place. It was like the scene of a hit and run accident after the victim has been rushed to hospital: on the faces wandering around there were looks of anxiety and attentiveness, but there would seem — to anybody stumbling onto the scene —no focus for the concentration and consternation.

On the first night of their arrival I was lingering in the safe, hoping that Alex would take the opportunity to join me to talk things over. After half an hour a familiar vast shadow did appear on the floor of the safe — but it was only Moira, tip-toeing in with the comically exaggerated steps of a cartoon Jerry creeping away from a Tom.

'Listen,' she whispered to me with mock vigilance. 'They're going to be ages out there. Mr Bentley's just opened a new bottle of smelling salts.' She handed me a little slip of pink paper. 'Do you think you could *steal* out quietly to get us all something to eat?' She produced a plastic bag from beneath her jumper. 'I'm not going to ask Mr Reid first because he'll just refuse.'

'Oh sure,' I said, taking the bag and slip of paper, grateful for the chance to get a change of scenery. Moira left the safe first to check that the coast was clear. A minute or two later she appeared at the door and gave me an exaggerated wink and I slipped out unnoticed by manager or accountant.

When I returned, the staff who weren't directly involved in checking anything swarmed over towards the few bare desks for the distribution of the food.

'Don't leave any of that rubbish for the cleaners,' Mr Reid said, no doubt having decided that his pretending to have authorized the visit to the shops was better in the eyes of the manager than any reprimand, which would only have revealed that the staff had been able to trick him. I glanced over at Alex, hoping to share the joke as usual, but he determinedly avoided my eyes.

That night I was shown other aspects of the characters and lives of the bank staff, as though the light which revealed them to me throughout the day had suddenly changed its angle, casting new shadows. Phone calls were made home to husbands, wives, lovers, parents. Those phone calls, carried out in the awful stillness of an office deprived of the babble of customers and machines, revealed much about the lifestyles of the staff outside the office — whether it was John Whiteman's whining conversation with his mother (he was obviously even more of a mummy's boy than we had suspected), or Roy's emotionless twenty-second bulletin to his wife, reinforcing the rumours of impending divorce.

As the night wore on, more and more of the staff, no longer needed by the auditors, gathered in one corner of the office and there occurred a sense that the departure from our daily routines required a similar departure in the form and content of our conversations. Perhaps this was simply due to the fact that we were all huddled together (optimistically clad in coats and scarves), on tables and chairs which formed the sociological semi-circle of the self-help groups; perhaps it was due to the confined silence which stimulated revelation like the silence of the confessional. Most of the staff chatted at length about subjects which were normally avoided: Beeny spoke about her father's drinking; Roy added a few brushstrokes to the black picture he painted of his home life; Ann was drawn into detailed descriptions of her life in Shettleston: the poverty, the dirt, the drudgery. Eventually even I was dragged into the conversation with a half-hearted moan about the lack of amenities in Woodhaven.

At the end of the week Alex and me were summoned into Mr Bentley's office. 'Don't be frightened by the numbers,' he said as we were led over to seats surrounded by four huge auditors who resembled bloodthirsty CIA officers as they towered above us.

They wanted to know why there were so many transfers of funds between our two accounts and why some withdrawals from my account had been obtained with slips forged by Alex and vice-versa. All of this was entirely innocent: I would borrow from Alex when he was in funds and I wasn't; he would withdraw money from me by forging slips if I wasn't at work on a particular day — but it was impossible to explain this to the auditors without revealing the extent of our relationship.

I was annoyed at this invasion of privacy. And frightened: it was impossible, with the two strangers staring down at us, not to feel as though we were already convicted criminals.

'I wasn't aware that the private transactions of members of staff were investigated in such detail,' I said. My face was red, throat dry. Alex was staring at his knees.

'It's standard procedure,' one of the inspectors said, glancing over at the manager who flashed me a how-long-have-you-been-in-the-bank look. Now I felt like a fool as well as a criminal.

'There's no witch-hunt going on,' Mr Bentley said, looking at me then at Alex. 'All the staff accounts — including my own — have been looked into in the same way.'

'And will you too be given the third degree over every innocent transaction you make?' There was a soft bump against the door. I wondered how many of them were listening.

'What business is it of yours who I give money to and who gives it to me?'

One of the inspectors picked up a file from the manager's desk, flicked through it as he spoke.

'It's nobody's business — unless there is some suspicion of irregularity in the transactions.'

I wished Alex would raise his head and explain. It wouldn't be the same if I had to.

'I still don't see why you should have the power to go around poking your nose into people's accounts trying to work out whether their every transaction is legitimate or not. What is it that is so unusual about someone lending money to someone else?'

The inspector with the folder raised his voice a little.

'It's not just the fact that transfers took place, it's the amounts, the frequency of them, and the dates.'

'What about the dates?'

Mr Bentley intervened. 'We're not accusing you of anything Paul, but the fact is that on some occasions amounts paid into your account by Alex, or vice-versa, have tallied with amounts that one of the tellers was short that day.'

Alex finally looked up, but still said nothing.

'But that's bound to happen,' I said. 'It's always fives, tens or twenties we borrow and pay back, and it's always fives, tens and twenties that tellers are short.'

'And the forged slips?'

'We gave each other permission to do that.' I looked round at Alex. He was staring at a Royal Bank calendar on the wall. When he realised that we were all waiting for him to speak he turned and nodded. Guiltily. Then he hung his head again: yes, your honour, we did commit the awful deed; but he led me on, you understand.

The auditors looked back and forth from Alex to me. I waited for them to ask the question I'd been eager to answer throughout the trial: why would two workmates be so free with each other's accounts? I was convinced it was that irregularity more than any other that was the reason for their suspicions. But the question was never asked.

'Well, that'll do for now,' one of them said at last, and we were let go.

I made no attempt to get Alex to apologise for his silence. The following Monday I complained indignantly to Mr Bentley about our treatment, using the incident as the excuse I had been waiting for to resign from the bank.

Security

Pat and I moved into his council flat in the East End of Glasgow on the same day late in August — almost a year since I joined the bank. We hired a big van and collected his things first from his mother's house. The bulk of his belongings consisted of two bookcases full of books and magazines. Fortunately he had few other possessions because nothing had been packed away.

'I didn't want to tempt fate by packing all my stuff away,' he told me when he saw my look of disbelief at his unreadiness. 'I can't believe that anything important is going to occur in my life until the moment it actually happens.' Later he changed his story and said that he would have just felt lonely — even for a few nights — without all his little accoutrements around him, with all his posters and paintings taken down from the walls. I could see what he meant: once the room was stripped bare, it looked as sad and miserable as a dog peering out of the window of an empty house.

Some of the paintings were Pat's own, as were the poems, written in coloured felt-tip pen and incorporated into a collage of black and white photographs of film and pop idols which covered one entire wall of his bedroom. I got the impression that the real reason Pat hadn't done any packing

was that he wanted me to see all the paintings and poems —
his life until then — before it was all packed away for good.

There was only one poem that I thought I understood —
about a little colony of frogs, all of whom changed colour as
they grew older, from black to grey — all except one who
turned green and yellow: this beautiful green frog was sad
because it wasn't grey like the others, so it used to cover
itself in mud to disguise its true colour — but even then it
wasn't happy. Only when it died and reverted to its original
black was it finally content. Pat eventually stopped handing
me poems to read when I persisted in comparing them to
that one.

He left his mother, who looked as though she must have
been in her seventies, with the promise that he would come
back to stay a few nights every week until she got used to
living alone. She just nodded and told us to have a nice time,
hardly aware of what was going on.

After we left Pat's house we drove to Woodhaven to
collect my hi-fi and the rest of the stuff I had left there
when I moved into Glasgow. I wanted to get away from
home completely before my parents discovered that I'd left
the bank. God knows what they would think of that.

I had been a bit apprehensive about their meeting Pat,
but it all worked out marvellously. He had toned down
the skinhead look for the occasion, wearing soft brown
cords and a white crew-neck with long sleeves to hide the
tattoos. My parents were obviously grateful to meet one
of those mysterious Glasgow friends they'd heard so little
about — and such a nice well-mannered one at that. With
Pat's baby-blond, shy-eyed fragility (I told him that one
of his tattoos should read 'This way up'), he had a head
start with my appearance-conscious parents, but he could
easily turn on the charm too — he was only too happy
to participate in the sort of banal conversation I found it
impossible to get involved in: one minute helping my mother
choose wallpaper designs, the next the expert driver discussing the roads with my father.

Before we got down to emptying my room, we all sat
down together for tea — the first meal I had taken with my
parents for years. Pat became even more of a hit with my

mother when he complimented her on the new Persian cat she had bought, which, curled up in its basket like a cloud of candy floss, was twitching its nose, sniffing food in the air.

'You should get away more,' he told my parents, when he discovered that they rarely went on holiday. 'You'll appreciate the house more if you go away and come back to it.' He could say the sort of things to them that I would have found it impossible to do: it would have been like suddenly commenting on a picture that had hung on a wall, uncriticised for years.

I let Pat and my father load the van while I packed things into their boxes: they were like father and son.

'Smile!' Pat would say every time he caught me alone. After we'd loaded the van I took him on a tour of Woodhaven, pointing out all the landmarks that he insisted on photographing with his expensive camera: Pat showed all the interest in my life that I had wanted Alex to. I popped into the local pub for the first time ever. It was actually quite pleasant looking inside (God knows what I was expecting), with a huge open log fire in the lounge, and a very cheap, comprehensive jukebox.

'Why did you ever move from here?' Pat said. When our family first moved to Woodhaven I found the silence and emptiness of the place eerie compared with the noise of Glasgow. But Pat was transfixed by it all.

I had to drag him past the cavalcades of sweet-smelling flowers so dazzlingly coloured that the senses reeled. After his drab East End neighbourhood, whose various shades of grey were only brightened by the graffiti, Woodhaven must have seemed like another Oz to Pat. As he bent over the wild violets, luscious lilacs and outrageously red roses, he seemed to expect them to burst into life and extend a Disney hand towards him.

'You're seeing it for the first time,' I told Pat. 'Imagine living here for five years with hardly any friends, nobody to talk to.' But he wasn't convinced. 'What is there in Glasgow that this place doesn't have? — The scene?' He said the word like a Communist saying 'Profit'. Pat hated the gay scene. I went over to the bar, not wanting to get caught up in that sort of argument again.

When I was at the bar I had a look around the pub, recognizing faces from the church, the street, St James. I saw people I hadn't seen in years. In the brawniest bodies and roughest faces I could still distinguish the relics of the tiny twelve-year-olds that roamed the streets when I first arrived there.

'Are you Linda Dobson's wean?' Pat asked me, gleefully imitating the Lanarkshire accent.

'That was my mother's maiden name,' I told him. He duly nodded over to the woman who had asked him. He was loving this. 'It's all just like one big happy family,' he said.

I felt terrible the next morning as we were leaving. Finally emptying my room of all its possessions seemed to make the occasion more momentous than when I had actually left home months before. This was the sort of emotional scene which neither my parents nor I were equipped for, so that Pat had to act out all the parts for us.

'Well, we'll certainly be back to visit you often,' he said, as my parents stood at the doorway. 'I'm sure that Paul's room will always be kept free for him.' My mother nodded. 'I'll make sure he comes to no harm in Barrowfield, don't you worry.' Then as we drove off: 'We'll send you a postcard when we get there!'

'Why didn't you say a proper goodbye when we left?' Pat asked me when we got onto the road out of Woodhaven. 'You just jumped into the van and waved.'

'We're not that type of family,' I said. 'It's their fault, not mine.'

After we'd driven on a bit he said: 'You should tell them you're gay: I think they would be alright about it. My mother was great after the initial shock. I think it's always easier for working-class parents to accept: they don't have as many ambitions for their children, or as many appearances to keep up, as the other lot.'

'Well, we'll soon find out,' I said.

'What do you mean?'

'I left a copy of *Gay Times* in one of my drawers — they'll probably think I left it there by mistake.'

'Isn't that a bit cowardly?'

'I think it's considerate: I want them to react without my presence there to influence them.'

'I still think it's a bit of a cop-out,' Pat said.

'But surely the "initial shock" isn't the important thing — why should I subject us all to that when it's the long-term reaction which is most important. I'm giving them a chance to consider their response before they present it to me. If they blew up in front of me, it might have made it impossible for us to communicate in the future.'

It began to rain. The pattering on the roof of the van, and the hazy look it gave to the world outside was so soporific that the conversation quickly petered out. Pat mumbled a few half-sentences — 'can't believe you're actually moving in — those gardens — that little gnome.' Then we both drifted into silence.

All the activity had driven thoughts of Alex and the bank from my mind. I hadn't thought about him all throughout the entire visit apart from a brief half-second when my mother mentioned the bank: it was like a sharp knife going straight through me, the wound sealing up behind it. And I would feel another stab when the van passed the bank — we were travelling along the same route as the bus. Such minor sufferings, though, couldn't compare with the agonies I'd suffered in the weeks just after Alex and I had split up. The first week was the worst: I couldn't seem to escape from his presence no matter where I went in the office. His aftershave lingered in every corner; in the safe I would continually come across scraps of paper and slips with his writing on them; and in the tearoom the familiar smell rising from his raincoat as it dried hung in the air threatening to choke me to death.

Things improved by the second week though: once Alex realised that I wasn't going to make any effort to get back together with him, he became a lot friendlier, asking how I was getting on with my swimming and weight-training. The third week after I'd handed in my resignation was even better: I was astounded by his reaction when he finally found out that I would be leaving the bank: he totally ignored me for two days. I felt an uplifting sense of power to think that I could so affect him.

The rest of the staff were totally stunned by my resignation: I found it impossible to answer their questions about what I intended to do after I left, having no more idea than they had. All I wanted to do was escape from Alex, have a long rest and think about the future.

The last few days of that third week became intolerable. Alex, having recovered from the surprise of my resignation, the surprise of finding out that I wasn't going to wait and wait for his next move, began to make things difficult for me — inviting John to the *Black Stallion* every day and arriving back ten minutes late, or discussing plans with the others for an extra special Christmas party. The rest of the staff, realising that there had been some sort of split, never missed an opportunity to comment on how little time we now spent together compared with Alex's first few months in the bank.

Even worse than that though was when they exhibited the new respect they had for me — for someone who was actually proving to be as good as his word and resigning from the bank. They had all vowed at one time or another that they were leaving: next month, next year, next week — Mary had actually got as far as sitting on her chair with her coat on, arms folded, resolved to walk out there and then, until the others talked her out of it. It was unsettling being treated as an outsider, a relative returned from a long absence abroad. This approach was something Alex encouraged in the others.

Fearing some stunt by Alex, and not being able to face up to any more days of such an atmosphere, I took the last week of my resignation off sick.

I smiled victoriously at him on the way out that last Friday; he smiled back, looking confused by my expression, unaware that I had decided to deprive him of another five days of upsetting me. I had won a minor battle — but it was a Pyrrhic victory if ever there was one.

The East End of Glasgow looked far worse than I remembered it looking when I stayed there as a child. I felt uneasy the minute Pat and I arrived in the neighbourhood he had managed to get a flat in: even though it was well after nine at night, the broken, litter-covered streets ('We should have hired a tractor not a van,' I said to Pat) were teeming with hordes of wild-looking youths. I felt even worse when we reached Pat's house: he was staying in the very dregs of the scheme.

'They make documentaries about this street,' I mumbled to him as we got out of the van. The minute we pulled up outside the house, a crowd gathered to watch the show. We had thought that it would be dark and quiet by the time we arrived, allowing us to sneak all our belongings into the house unnoticed — but it was still infuriatingly bright, and the streets were as busy as George Square just after the discos shut. We were forced to lock the van door behind us every time we took an item up to the house, and then to lock the house door behind us on the return trip — for there was a crowd gathering there too.

Every bundle we carried out of the van was speculated on by the dangerous-looking youths who surrounded us, and everything correctly identified ('Look — they've got a video'), even though we had taken great pains to disguise all our more valuable belongings beneath curtains and blankets. It had all gone very wrong: we had hoped to sneak in with the minimum fuss, and thereafter try hard not to draw any attention to ourselves. But we had become the talking point of the street within an hour of our arrival.

Pat left to return the van to the friend he'd borrowed it from. I tried a light in the house: no electricity. Before the light began to fade I took a good look around all the rooms. The place was a wreck. The previous owner had dumped all his rubbish in the middle of the floor of every room in the house. There were piles of smelly old clothes, empty paint tins, ancient newspapers, and even heaps of ashes spread across the floors. Every fitting that could be wrenched off the wall had been taken away.

As the darkness closed in around me, I felt miserable. There was a bang at the door and I jumped up happily, thinking it was Pat. Children were peering through the letter-box.

'Wan a' thim's stull there!' a voice shouted when it saw me coming down the hall. They ran away laughing, in the knowledge that they could always try again another day. I looked at all my possessions scattered across the bare concrete floor, at records broken in the mad rush to get everything safely inside, and felt total despair: no job, no Alex, and the prospect of living in this dump as the only certainty in the future.

I looked down onto the streets that my mother and I had passed quickly through sometimes on the way into the city centre: the comical 'gardens' were still there, with their weed jungles and pathetic stumps of baby trees; and the graffiti still flourished: it was almost a tribal history of the neighbourhood with its endless scorings out, paintings over and lurid amendments — 'Tongs Rule Ya Bass 1974' in faded blue, was almost obliterated by 'Tongs ruled, Spurs Supreme!' in day-glo green.

I almost burst into tears when I saw Pat coming up the street towards the house. Although he was still in the distance, I easily recognized the short blond figure and the erratic walk. As he got closer, I could see that he was holding an ice-cream cone in each hand as he meandered through the hostile crowds, not realising how vulnerable he was. Smiling beatifically in his green GI shirt, he looked like a young soldier, innocently strolling through a minefield. When he arrived in the house, the mood changed entirely: he brought food (hamburgers and chocolate), drink (cans of strong lager), and light (the mains hadn't been switched on, he noticed). Suddenly the place looked a little more comfortable: it was ours after all. That first night we lay together on a double mattress on the floor, too tired to assemble the bed. As we listened to the menacing growls of the boys in the street ('Naebody gets their hole every night in Blackpool — ye might get a burd but no yer hole'), we were frightened and aroused in equal measure. We drifted off into a nervous, fitful sleep, both wrapped around each other, legs entwined, hand clutching hand, bum snuggled up against crotch, in an attempt to create contact in as many places as possible.

If I awoke in the night and looked outside there was always some sign of activity — a pair of boys lounging against a wall, waiting; or simply a middle-aged, washed-out-looking woman peering out of a window on the street opposite. It was as though the scheme was sick with fever and found it impossible to surrender to the cool, deep, well-earned slumber of the West End city I'd given up.

The first thing we did next day was to buy a good strong lock for the front door. As I assembled the lock, several boys stopped on the landing to offer advice (and peer into the flat). I tried to be as friendly as my nervousness would allow: the boys were laden down with leather, chains and safety pins — even their garish Mohican hairstyles looked like offensive weapons. Our next door neighbour, a woman in her early forties, appeared at the top of the stairs, exhausted from carrying two bags of groceries up them, but not too tired to chase the boys away.

'Right! Fuckin' doon the stairs!' she shouted. 'Ye've awe goat yer ain closes tae ston in!' The boys trundled down the stairs, bellowing back 'Fuckin' cow!' when they got to the bottom. The woman rested her bags on the landing as she opened her door.

After so many years away from Glasgow's East End I was continually surprised at how foreign I found the voices. The accent used to be so familiar — something I could slip in and out of for teachers or other adults — but I would have felt like an imposter if I spoke it now. Pat went easily into slang with his mother. I wondered if he felt relaxed with me.

'Christ that'll no dae ye much good!' she said when she saw the lock I was installing. 'Ma door's been put in twice: it's a new door you're needing to get.' She tapped at her own door, which sounded solid and metallic. I had wondered why there were so many new, unpainted doors throughout the close. The next day Pat showed me a pile of empty syringes and crisp packets filled with wads of glue that he had found on the landing. Nevertheless, we tried to ignore the warning bells going off in our heads: we were here now —so we might as well try to make the most of it.

We went round the house, methodically listing all the things that needed to be done by the council. The final list was a mile long: I could see now how Pat had managed to get a council house without spending any time on the waiting list.

It was soon obvious that I would have to do the majority of the electrical and carpentry work — Pat was useless at that sort of thing, being too impatient to see a finished product to do any job properly. He liked to watch me work, fetching scissors and nails for me, and handing them over like a nurse handing a scalpel to a surgeon. He would try to irritate me by kneeling on the floor in front of me, his head resting on the ground, watching carefully and eagerly, like a dog expecting a bone to be thrown.

My father turned up at the flat at the end of September. I was less embarrassed about the fact that he was looking at me for the first time as a homosexual than about the state the flat was in. Although Pat and I had spent all our free time, in the five weeks we'd been there, trying to knock the place into shape, it was nowhere near being finished. All our calculations regarding time and money had proved to be wildly optimistic. It was going to take far longer and cost much more than we could afford to get the place sorted out. And money was short: we were having to make do on my unemployment benefit and Pat's wages from the off licence. The council had proved as inefficient as we had feared: in all the time we'd been there, they had made no start to any of the repairs that were necessary. The closest we'd come to that was the delivery of a huge bag of plaster, which had been dumped in the middle of the living room, where it would stay until the arrival of the plasterers — whenever that would be. It was this monstrosity which my father used as a prop to divert attention from his nervousness, as he said what he'd come to say.

'How do you think we felt,' he said, strolling round the mountain of plaster, kicking at it with his toes. 'Couldn't you at least have had the courage to tell us to our faces?'

'And that would have made all the difference then?' I said sarcastically. I had always planned in my mind that this inevitable confrontation would be conducted in a calm and reasonable tone, but I was so disgusted with his behaviour towards Pat — he had ignored him from the minute he stepped into the flat, and was still turning his back on him every time he stood in front of him — that I found it impossible to control myself. I gave my father the same answer I had given Pat to explain my actions, my temper becoming more and more uncontrollable, the more I looked at Pat's dejected face: the snub seemed doubly sinful, since it had been Pat who had shown faith in my father's intelligence.

'If it's guilt or an apology you're after then you're wasting your time. As far as I'm concerned the only person who's committed a sin around here is you —'

'And how do you make that out?'

'What else do you call blind prejudice?'

He got up to go. Pat let him out. When he came back he told me he'd asked him if it would be all right if we still visited Woodhaven.

'We've got to leave *some* lines of communication open,' he said.

As Pat and I lay in bed that night, I considered just how important he had become to me. I had enjoyed the five weeks we'd been together immensely: that period conformed exactly to the image I had in mind of what monogamy would be like. Everything I had enjoyed doing by myself up until then — watching TV, eating meals, walking in the park — became doubly pleasurable. I got so used to being with Pat every minute of the day that if he stepped outside for an errand I began to feel lonely. This dependence worried me — not least because I didn't want Pat to suffer the same dependence on me.

From the first day that we moved into the flat, Pat and I had avoided the gay scene: he because he hated it, me to avoid Alex. As a consequence, we had, so far, never had any confrontation about the state of our relationship. In theory we were room-mates. I had warned Pat before I agreed to be his 'lodger' that although I knew it was inevitable that we would sleep together, I was not yet ready for monogamy.

'I haven't had the same chance that you and Alex have had to experiment on the gay scene,' I said. 'I was only on the scene a few weeks before I got involved with Alex.'

'Oh, yes,' Pat agreed, 'it's a big house after all — big enough for us both to lead separate lives in it — as long as we're both careful.' But from the moment we arrived there we had been living like a married couple.

I wasn't at all sure that this was what I wanted. I cursed the black-hearted Cupid that had led me to that job in Rosehill: surely if I hadn't met Alex I would have been more than content with Pat? Or was it simply a matter of loving and not loving? Would I still have felt the urge, despite my feelings for Pat, to find out if there was something more? I felt that while I shut myself away like this with him, I was shunning any threats to our relationship. Sooner or later I would have to confront Alex and the rest of the gay scene: only then would I be able to place our relationship in perspective.

I began to take the opportunity, while Pat stayed overnight with his mother during the week, to go back out on the scene alone.

Pat found out a month later. I left the house at eight as usual, an hour after he went round to his mother's, leaving two lights on in the house, and the radio playing in the living room. I was always nervous about leaving the flat as I passed the surly youths on the landing. It was surely only a matter of time before someone realised that the house was empty. Often when Pat and I were playing records the boys outside would bang on the door and ask us to turn the music up so they could hear it as they sniffed and snorted their brains away on the landing (Pat and I soon found out that, as we had suspected, ours was one of the main shooting and glue-sniffing closes).

'Won't the neighbours complain?' I would ask innocently.

'Not if they know what's good for them,' I was told. 'They're all feart of this close.'

When I left the house that night they asked again. I told them that it was the radio Pat was listening to, and it wouldn't go any louder.

'Hiv ye no goat any Led Zep or Kiss?' one of them asked as I made my way down the stairs.

'Led Zeppelin!' the others mocked him. 'Yer a fuckin' heid-banger!'

'And you're a wanker!'

'Yer da's a spastic!'

'Yer ma's a whore!'

When I got to the bottom of the stairs one of them shouted down, 'Hey, we hivny seen the photos yet!'

'They haven't come back from the chemist,' I shouted back. Pat and I had met a crowd of the Barrowfield mob in the Green when we were out there taking photographs one day. We were only too happy to oblige them by taking snaps of them in various poses, which to them were hilarious, to us intensely erotic — especially since they were all half-naked and sweating from their exertions on the football field. So far so good: as far as keeping on their good side, we had got off to a good start. But this sort of camaraderie was tentative at best: I had already heard some of them out on the landing speculating about the set-up of our household ('Hiv eny of youze ever seen any burds goin' in there?').

As usual I had two very quick whiskies when I reached the pub. There was so much tension to get out of my system: worry about leaving the house empty, guilty feelings about going behind Pat's back; anxiety about how I would react to Alex if he should pop in later. The first time I met him after I began going out alone again had been worse than expected. There was no way I could avoid being near him: I knew so few people on the gay scene that the only alternative to joining his company was standing alone a few feet away from him, like a fool. Besides, the main reason I had began going out at all was to try to exorcise Alex from my consciousness, to live through that one last thing which would put an end to it all. Despite the fact that I felt so uncomfortable, I was determined to stick it out.

But the sight of Alex mooning over his new friend was unendurable. Watching them together, talking and joking in that exclusive language that only two people at any one time can understand, I felt the same sort of despair that a divorced parent must feel on seeing his only child clinging to its new parents. Despite everything that had happened, I still thought of Alex as mine and only mine.

Gradually, though, those encounters began to have less effect on me. Alex made attempts, every time I met him, to make me feel jealous or unsettled. This had the opposite effect on me: they only showed that, no matter how much attention he lavished on his new boyfriend (reaching new heights of Cartlandesque embarrassment that surpassed even John and Rose — who would never have dared maintain a kiss for ten seconds let alone ten minutes) he still couldn't take my presence for granted.

Alex hadn't arrived by ten o'clock that night at the end of October, which meant that he wasn't going to be there: I could relax.

'Have you ever been in love?' I asked the so-so-looking man who had sidled up beside me and started a conversation. It was a question I had asked everybody I had gone home with, eager to discover in their experience some indication of what it was I felt for Alex and Pat, hopeful that someone could tell me which was most worth while.

Mark, the man I was talking to, was not very attractive, but bravely optimistic. His clothes were too stylish for his podgy frame: he was wearing a labrador-yellow sweat shirt which screamed desperately and pathetically for attention, like advertising hyperbole on second-hand goods. He may as well have embroidered The Legendary Mark across his chest.

'God, does it show?' he replied in answer to my question. Luckily Mark was a brooder, a thinker and a talker. Some of the people I'd spoken to seemed to have drifted through life, from one crisis to another, without ever stopping to analyse their situation to help them avoid any traumas in the future. That type was no good to me. Mark had thought through his mistakes endlessly; his story came gushing out fluently and articulately.

I went along with him to the disco, an hour earlier than anyone else — at my insistence: I wanted the upper hand in the proceedings. I had become rather cynical about cruising since I had started going back out alone again. Getting in early allowed me to view everyone as they poured into the disco: I was able to study closely their various states of confidence or nervousness, as well as their physical attributes.

Which was an Alex, which was a Pat — that was really what I was interested in.

I bumped into Sammy as Mark and I came off the dance floor later in the night. I had met him three weeks previously. The first words he had said to me were 'You must drink a lot of milk' while squeezing my, by then, firm rounded biceps. Sammy only drank in *The Waterloo*, and was most definitely Rough.

'You're looking great,' he said to me that night, grabbing my crotch and peering into my eyes. Sammy was anything but subtle. I introduced him to Mark, but only after accepting his compliments and buttering him up a bit: he was dangerously slow and liable to explode into violence if not treated properly.

As Mark and he made a desultory conversation I began to look around the hall at all the faces, all the types, and it struck me how difficult it was going to be to become involved with anyone again: even the most mundane task of all — finding a body for the night was strewn with pitfalls. Finding a face that fitted the image of acceptability in the mind was only the first step: more often than not, the personality did not fit the face. Before I heard Sammy speak, as I watched him from afar the first night I saw him in the disco, I had supposed him to be a lawyer or a doctor, due to the expensive-looking suit he wore, and his tidy appearance. It was only when he turned up a week later, in torn jeans and a dirty white T-shirt that I went home with him and found out he was a labourer: the suit was for a court appearance that day.

There were so many familiar faces now that it was strange to remember how, not so long ago, I had thought the Glasgow gay scene so big and unmanageable. All the regulars were there: Black Marlena — androgynous Indian beauty (was it a girl or a guy?) in suit and tie; the man in his fifties who always danced by himself, swishing a red cape around as though he were taunting an imaginary bull; and the fashion queens, acting out all the videos to the pop songs blasting from the speakers, working so hard at enjoying themselves and looking cool (by the end of the night they would have rejected every potential partner with an icy stare, waiting for Mr Worthy-of-me, only to go home with the first person who asked — regardless of looks, age or intelligence — when the lights came up).

The fact that 'the scene' was small suited everybody: there was only ever one disco open at a time on any particular night, so no worries about what you might be missing elsewhere; and all the bars were within easy walking distance of each other. This meant that people drifted from one to another, often several times a night. *The Waterloo*, because it was on a busy shopping street and open to the sun, was busy early on in the day; when it got dark, people made their way to *The Vintners* and *Squires*. Because it was such a small collective of gay people that circulated round the pubs and discos it seemed to operate intuitively, like one huge organism: new establishments were flocked to and deserted en masse; transsexuals and transvestites always marginalized themselves (or were marginalized by everybody else) into the less reputable places; and there was only ever one lesbian bar at any particular time, because of the relatively smaller numbers. Although everyone always *said* they preferred mixed male/female (and most of the intelligent ones did), there was not much point in the women going to half a dozen places where they knew they would be outnumbered twenty to one when there was one place they knew all their friends would be; and the single males only ever went where 'the men' were.

Sammy was mocking the camper elements in the crowd. 'Look at them all in their best frocks,' he said disgustedly. I dragged him up to dance to the first camp record that came on: *You always hurt the one you love*.

'Shouldn't that be the other way round?' I said to him when we were on the dance floor. He looked over at the record spinning on the DJ's turntable. 'Will I ask him to turn it over?' he said.

'No. I mean the one you love always hurts you.' But he only started expressing that paranoid, confused look until I kissed it away.

When we returned to Mark, a man in his forties was talking to him. Immediately we came over, he broke off the conversation and began to back away. 'Well, I'll leave you young chaps alone. You don't want me cramping your style.'

'God, I hate that sort of self-pitying crap,' I said to Mark when the man had gone.

'Oh, Colin's got his problems,' Mark said. 'How would you feel if you came in here and you were his age.'

'He's only in his forties for God's sake.'

'How many guys is he going to get at that age in here though?'

'But how many girls would he get if he were straight? Why is it gays blame every problem they have on being gay? If Colin were straight he would probably be married to a forty-year-old woman. Would he be any happier? Certainly not sexually.'

'Yes, perhaps we've come to expect too much from each other,' Mark said. Why is it that articulate liberalism is such a sexual turn-off? Since I didn't feel like having my cock chewed black and blue by Sammy that night, I slipped away while they were on the dance floor, embarrassed as always at the banal appropriateness of the Hi-Energy soundtrack to my exit ('Thank God, there's always tomorrow — because tonight my man's not here — oh no.').

On the way home, as usual when I was alone, I regretted that I didn't have a partner with me as I passed all the dishevelled sexuality of the similarly unlucky straight boys pouring out of the discos: all that sexual energy going to waste.

I passed a girl who was standing in the middle of the street with a vaguely solicitous look. I wondered if she was a prostitute. But as I got closer, I could see that she was waiting for her boyfriend, who was pissing in the street against a wall, his hot stream creating new continents on the map of vomit beside him, a landscape made three dimensional when he dropped a bag of chips onto it. The girl began to hiccup and I felt sick.

'I've just been to the doctor's,' Pat told me, when he returned the next day.

'Oh, not your mother I hope,' I said.

'No — only this,' he said, holding up his index finger.

'What's wrong with it?' I said innocently. Then I saw the hideous little insect crawling about on it.

'Crabs!' Pat said furiously. There was no reasoning with him. No matter how much I reminded him of our non-monogamy pact he still branded me as some kind of monster.

'But you can't say that I'm immoral because I don't want to be monogamous with you at this stage,' I protested. 'I don't blame Alex for not loving me,' I said, with all the conviction of the bare-faced liar. 'That's life.'

'Alex and you were a different thing entirely.'

'I can't see that: to my mind it all comes back to the same thing: pursuer and pursued.'

'So what do we do now?'

'Surely that's up to you to decide. I'll move out if you want me to.'

'But what do you want to do?'

'Go on the way we have been going on — but if that's not good enough for you . . .'

I was asking him to wait for the next thing, like Alex had done to me.

'You know the situation. You knew how I felt about Alex.'

'Alex has nothing to do with us,' Pat screamed, banging his radio alarm against the table — after which it began to play its irritating waking tune — two octaves higher.

The argument was eventually ended by a knock on the door. It was the father of one of the boys whose photo we'd taken.

'I don't want the likes of you taking photos of any of my boys again. Okay?'

The next day a brick came through the kitchen window.

.

Disaster

The sun's high noon made a white star of the metal window of a deserted office block in the centre of the city. From where I was lying, covered with old discarded carpets and curtains, in a long cardboard box in the waste-ground opposite the building, I realised that I was the only person in the world who could see this star. The street that the building towered over was brisk with lunchtime workers, newly escaped from nearby office blocks, but none of these passers-by would see the star, even if they bothered to stop and look up, something they seemed incapable of doing as they zig-zagged past each other like accelerated chess pieces. Anyone wanting to see the star would have to be in my exact position, lying in the old cardboard box at the precise angle I was. Even then he would have to half-close one eye and move his head as slowly as the invisible movements of the hands of a clock in order to follow the brilliance of the star as the sun's progress across the sky twisted it further and further from his line of vision. Somehow it seemed important to me that I keep sight of this star: it had been the first thing I had noticed when I woke up.

The familiar hangover pounding in my head told me that I must have been drunk when I collapsed there —

although drunkenness itself was not adequate explanation for my having spent the night on a dirty waste-ground in the middle of the city. Drunk or not, I had never ever fallen asleep outside. The reflex and intuition of the habitual drunkard had always guided me home safely. I may have then lost consciousness halfway through some greasy take-away, awakening hours later, fully clothed, to a square of television interference, but I always awoke safely indoors.

That's why on awakening I believed that I was at home: the white star was surely the bedside lamp, fumbled on half-consciously, surprising me with its brightness as usual; and when I heard the voices of the passers-by, I experienced that curious sensation that I always did on awakening to Pat's radio alarm: the voices and music seemed to suggest that I had been listening to them for hours, and yet I was fully aware that I had just woken. As soon as I realised that the voices were coming from people hundreds of yards away from me, they seemed to dim from a roaring accusation to a manageable hum, in the same way that Pat's radio alarm did as I gained consciousness.

I had been staring uncritically, unquestioningly at the star for some time, in the same way that I had stared at the bedside lamp or the cracks in the ceiling on so many post-pub, post-disco mornings, suffering the presence of alcohol in my stomach, hoping to drift back to sleep before the bladder demanded immediate attention, when I began to realise that my senses were beginning to disappear one by one, the way squares of light do from the front of a house as night falls and the inhabitants gradually drift off to bed. I knew that my mouth must be coated with alcohol — there was an empty bottle of gin on the ground next to me, lying lop-sided in the snow like a sinking ship — but I could no longer taste it. I could no longer smell the frost in the air, although I could see the snow lying thick on the ground — for the first time in my life seeming not protective but threatening, like a fleet of poisonous doves. Neither could I feel the cold on my skin, although I could see the breath escaping from my lungs in slow, rhythmic pulses, like steam from a train that had just begun to move — or was about to stop. When the hum of the passers-by disappeared too, the only sense I was left with was the one which had brought me to consciousness: sight.

Thank God in a way. Thank God. At least the pain had gone at last: the cold had frozen numb the bruises on my arms and legs, and the alcohol no longer stung the cuts on my mouth, nor did tears pain me if they invaded the wound in my eye. But where had these marks come from?

Had I fallen, been stabbed or worse?

While the white star was shining there was still hope: one of the rooms was still occupied. But it was surely only a matter of time before this square too disappeared, leaving total darkness. I had never intended this cardboard box to be my coffin, but there was some last trace of rationality in me that warned that if I didn't react in some way to my situation — and soon — then I would sink into oblivion.

The white star disappeared. At that same moment as the mundane office block became recognizable (I was in Harper Street), I began to remember.

Pat and I had had an argument the day before — our first major blow-up in the four weeks since he discovered that I was going out behind his back. I had been lying in bed, nursing the beginnings of a cold with the remains of a bottle of Malibu that Pat had stolen from the off-licence he worked part-time at. As I listened to the metrical music of the melting snow dripping down from the cracks in the ceiling that the council still hadn't repaired, I became aware that there was a new rhythm to the drops that day — a drip-drip-drip-plunk, as opposed to the familiar drip-drip-drip. This additional leak I eventually mentally traced to the cupboard that Pat kept his books in. It vaguely occurred to me that Pat's books might be getting wet, but I was so warm and cosy beneath the sheets with my drink that I managed to convince myself that the drips were — yes, the drips were definitely splattering off the floor, and not the shelves, so Pat's books were safe, and I could continue to lay in bed, as the dampness which was collecting on the carpet spread towards me.

Pat was furious when he returned from work to find half his books soaked useless.

'I know you don't have an ounce of literary appreciation,' he screamed at me, 'but to lie there and let this happen. Christ!'

'I do have literary appreciation,' I said stupidly, slightly drunk from the Malibu. 'I like science fiction.'

'Science fiction,' Pat snorted derisively. 'Don't you think you live in enough of a dream world?'

'What do you mean?'

'Trying to find another Alex.'

'That's garbage,' I said. 'I just don't want monogamy yet.'

'Is that why you drag yourself onto the scene every week?' This was the first reference Pat had made to my activities while he was at his mother's since the first argument, although there had been a few sulky atmospheres when he returned home after a night spent away.

'I've been out twice in the last month,' I told Pat truthfully, 'and both those times I've come home alone.' I had been going out less in recent weeks — not because of Pat's displeasure, nor for fear of leaving the house empty — things had been quieter since the brick through the window, the November cold having cleared the streets — but because the nights out had become so monotonous. 'I suppose I'm just becoming bored with the scene.'

'That's because you've got nothing else in your life but the pubs,' Pat said, emptying the cupboard of the wet books with a smile on his face now at my admission of discontent. 'The pubs should be somewhere to go after work, as an escape, an alternative, not a be-all and end-all in themselves.'

I got out of bed and started to get dressed. 'I'll dry the books off while you're at your mother's,' I said, changing the subject before he thought to remind me that it was about time I started to look for a job, something he had been hinting at recently.

I walked Pat as far as the bus stop on the way to his mother's.

'Do you really think it's wise to go swimming when you've got a cold coming on?' he said, as we stood freezing at the bus stop.

'It's the quickest way I know of clearing my sinuses,' I told him. 'Besides, there can't be an unhealthier atmosphere than one in a room soaking with dampness.' After Pat left, I decided to walk into town, drifting around Glasgow in a stupor, my head buzzing with antibiotics, Malibu and cough mixture, the aura of unreality made complete by the Walkman music resounding through my skull, almost as potent as alcohol for giving me a world of my own.

Boys were still playing football in the snowy streets, despite the temperature, jumpers tied around their waists as though it were the height of summer. Once I left the East End, I was suddenly reminded that Glasgow was 'Miles Better'. I somehow doubted that the recent mania for refurbishing rather than wrecking would apply to Barrowfield. If Glasgow was a beautifully patterned curtain, neglected for so long that it had gathered dirt and dust, then Barrowfield was the tattered frayed edge that was beyond repair, fit only for tearing off and disposing of.

When Pat and I had left the house, a snow as fine as salt had begun to fall from the sky; by the time I reached town it was whirling around my head like a cotton-wool tornado. I felt miserable at the prospect of returning to an empty house without Pat there to scold me for wandering the streets bare-headed with a cold. One of the best things about getting soaked was coming back home to a warm bath and having Pat dry my hair by the fire before a cosy drink together.

I nipped into *The Waterloo* to wait for the weather to ease up a bit: concerned more with personality than appearance, it was the only gay pub I was willing to show my face in in such a bedraggled state.

Alex was the last person I expected to see there.

'You're looking well,' he said. I was shivering in one of Pat's old denim jackets, my hair plastered flat against my forehead and covered in melting snow.

'Thanks,' I replied with no sarcasm in my voice, refusing to become embroiled in the old insult tango again. I nodded to the boy he was with on the way to the bar. When I got back, I was subjected to the usual update on the goings-on at the bank: Ann was engaged, Roy had begun divorce proceedings at last; Rose and John had split up then got back together again; a new junior had finally arrived.

'It sounds better than *Eastenders*,' David, the boy with Alex, said, with an eagerness to appear witty and interesting which was charming and saddening at the same time.

It was only later, when a stream of old favourites of Alex's and mine came over the jukebox that I experienced any surge of emotion. The mood inspired by the alcohol and the music was more evocative of Alex than his physical presence in front of me, a fact that seemed to underline to me how much of our relationship was based on illusion on my part.

'I put these on whenever I want to have a good cry,' Alex said. I didn't know whether to believe him or not: the mystery was still there — but it was a mystery I was no longer interested in solving.

'Have you ever felt so bad that you couldn't listen to a sad record?' I said. 'There is something worse than sentimental sadness you know.'

'Oh yes, I know!' He turned towards David. 'Some young drama queen slapping you in the face in a fit of temper for one thing!' The two smiled conspiratorially, the boy blushing happily at the reference to one of their little tiffs: just like real lovers!

But Alex's self-satisfied smile faded when he realised that I was about to leave. 'Of course I understand,' he said, turning his back on David, whose blushing face immediately drained white. 'You seem to imagine that you're the only one on earth ever to have felt —' he smiled as the jukebox furnished the appropriate phrase '— Love Pains.'

'I tried to tell you this before,' he moved closer, lowering his voice, 'but you hit me the last time.' I put my drink on the bar and folded my arms tightly, pantomiming placid fascination.

'I went through all the same traumas with Diane — wondering what she felt, how long it would last, trying to get onto some sort of safe secure plateau where I could relax in confidence. But when I did eventually get there — and even then it didn't last — I realised what I'd missed on the way.'

'But I thought Diane was after you as much as you were after her?'

'That's just the point: whether she was or not I wouldn't have known — I was like you: I had one thing in mind, one goal I was heading for that blinded me to anything that didn't conform to a step on the way to it. But while I was so busy trying to push us both onto the next step I was ignoring all the good things about being in love for the first time. Then, just when I began to feel secure, everything had become routine. That's the one thing that's worse than sentimental sadness for me — even worse than unrequited love: at least with that you've got an attainable goal — but innocence, by its very nature, is unattainable — as soon as you recognize what it is, you've lost it.'

'— in the very act of recognizing it,' I said. 'It's not that different from unrequited love you know.' There was a sad lack of tension in our discussion: we were at last beginning to speak the same language.

Alex's friend was chatting behind us. Anyone would have thought by the tone of his voice that he was interested above all else in the world in the weekend exploits of the barman he was talking to, but there was a hesitation in his speech, not easily observed — the hesitation of an expert piano player on an off night, only recognizable to other experts — which betrayed his concentration on Alex's conversation with me.

When the barman noticed the pause in our dialogue he leaned over and asked Alex if the baby had arrived yet.

'Any day now,' Alex said, seeming a little embarrassed: an indignant ripple of chatter circulated among the other customers.

'That was all your fault,' he said to me, pointing accusingly, the way he had done the day I didn't wash out his cup. 'The baby wasn't planned.'

'So?' I couldn't see what that had to do with me.

'So Diane thought perhaps this time we were drifting just a bit too far —'

'— I'm amazed she put up with this for so long,' I said. I could see where the conversation was going: on the one hand I was amazed and pleased at the revelations, on the other I knew that neither of us would have been able to give so much away unless we realised that there was nothing more to lose — or win.

'Oh, she had just as many affairs of her own, don't worry about her.'

'And after the baby's born?'

'No more of this.'

I glanced towards David. 'Just like that?'

'With any luck.' He jerked his eyebrows up in his forehead, imitating my own mannerism, as he had done at our very first meeting. We had travelled all that way along the tightrope only to hobble back stubbornly to the starting point: the end I was looking towards turned out to be the beginning.

Immediately Alex went to the toilet, David broke away from the person he was talking to. 'Do you still love him?' he asked me. The question was not put to me because I was considered a possible future rival — I could see that the boy was too shrewd to suspect that — but because David wanted to find out whether the disease he had caught had any cure.

'I don't know,' I replied wearily. I knew that nothing I said would be of any real value to him. 'But I know when I'm not happy.' I smiled. 'That's the most important question you have to ask yourself.'

I left the pub before Alex returned from the toilet.

On the way to the swimming pool I popped into the city museum: I hadn't visited it since I was a child at school. After all those years, my favourite exhibit was still there, and still my favourite. While all the other children were clustering round the prehistoric remains of the once rulers of the earth, I was gazing at the glass case containing the letters written from the battlefront by soldiers in the First World War. To my mind those letters were more awe-inspiring than any old dinosaur bones. Prehistoric remains created no image in my mind, but as I gazed at the yellowed letters, I gave their unknown authors faces and bodies and backgrounds: they were all young and handsome; they all died in battle; and they all had a lover waiting for them back home. I attempted to shine up the dull glass that separated me from the hazy words, but they remained, like the past itself, as Alex had said, vivid but untouchable.

The swimming pool was very busy, packed out with noisy kids from the local school. Tall, broad-shouldered fourteen-year-olds were wearing thin white football shorts with nothing beneath them but fully developed penises which thrashed about obscenely as they spurted up and down the pool indiscriminately and unpredictably — in marked contrast to the older swimmers who were diligently and methodically paddling across from side to side, counting the laps patiently as they did so.

Because the boys had been making such a commotion at the deep end, the girls had drifted down to the other side of the pool. Whenever a pair of boys or girls did venture outside their own territory, there was a tense, silent challenge exchanged between invader and invaded, then a sudden rush back to safety. It was exactly like the scene at the beginning of the school dances, when all the boys were lined up against one wall and all the girls against another, both sides too dependent on each other to risk humiliation by making the first move. Here, by their nakedness, the sexes were distinguished even more: barefoot, the females walked extra daintily, while the boys' masculine clumsiness was emphasised by the way they padded along, chests stuck out to maintain balance, arms dangling loosely by their sides, like monkeys.

I had been in the pool for about twenty minutes, picking up speed as I travelled from side to side counting the laps, when I realised that one of the schoolboys was pacing himself with me. I found this quite flattering, and made it obvious that I knew what he was doing. The pacing eventually became racing: the loser would be he who had to wait too long at the side to rest. The boy was a skinhead wth tattoos on each shoulder and black mascara, which was running down his cheeks in tribal streaks.

'I was just about to give in,' he said, when he finally won the race; we were floating at the edge of the pool, both breathing in and out deeply, exhilarated.

'Are you with the school party?' I asked him. He nodded, obviously embarrassed.

'The big man's coming to take us back, I think,' he said, looking up towards a tall burly man who was glancing frequently at his watch.

'He looks quite human for a teacher,' I said, remembering the sadistic gym teacher from St James.

'Oh, he's alright,' the boy said. 'Apart from the fact he's queer.'

With that, he dived off to join his friends at the deep end.

Thoroughly depressed, I headed for the showers before the schoolkids took them over. A boy smelling of fresh apples (soap or shampoo) was pissing furtively against the wall. 'Ouch!' he yelped, glancing round at me embarrassed. 'Soap in ma nob.'

There were two other people there: a man in his late twenties and his five-year-old son. The man was washing the boy's hair with bubbly shampoo, the boy squealing with delight every time his head was rinsed out under the jet of water.

'Can we have chicken curry tonight, daddy, can we?' the boy asked as the two of them left.

'You like that, don't you?' the father said, trying to catch my eye proudly as he passed. But I turned away. A wave of black depression engulfed me as I thought of Alex and Diane and the baby, and how useless my hopeless little affair with Alex was compared with that.

I walked home in a daze, staring at the ground, trying to think of nothing, only beginning to register my surroundings again when I reached home. It suddenly occurred to me as I climbed the stairs that the two boys who had passed by me were carrying Pat's record player and my radio. When I appeared in the hallway, a horde of teenagers and small children swarmed out of every room, like bees escaping an invaded nest. They flew down the stairs, still clutching whatever possessions of mine and Pat's they had managed to grab on the way.

I sat in the middle of the ruins, sipping at the bottle of gin that one of them had already been at, to calm my nerves. An hour later I left to report the break-in to the police. There was no way I could re-secure the lock on the door which had been smashed — but they had left nothing of value for anyone to steal anyway: the house had been defiled — it wasn't ours any more.

On the way to the police station I saw the two boys who had stolen the record player and radio.

'I want them back,' I said, bravely drunk enough to confront them. 'I want them back right now!'

They both looked at each other in mock, amused ignorance.

'What is it you want?' one of them said, raising a fist which had N.E.A.L. tattooed on the fingers. 'Is it this?'

Towards the End

'Who found me?'

'Nobody *found* you.' Pat's hand was resting on top of mine but separated from it by thick layers of hospital bedsheets.

'You walked into the Royal by yourself — Genito-Urinary Department by the way — don't you remember?'

I shook my head and told him what I was beginning to remember: staggering out of the waste-ground I'd woken up in and limping across town towards, apparently, the hospital. Memories were maddeningly vague though, only appearing in my mind slowly, in patches, like a photograph developing. Pat had been sitting by my side when I awoke: I'd been in hospital for two days.

'The house!' I shouted, suddenly remembering the break-in.

'It's not that bad,' Pat said. 'The police have managed to get a lot of the stuff back — we weren't exactly robbed by professionals.' As he spoke he surveyed my face, screwing up his own at my cuts and bruises. I was so full of painkillers that I didn't feel any suffering except through his eyes.

'I don't even remember being beaten up,' I said, smiling with Pat as he wiped away the slabber of blood seeping out of the cut on my mouth that reopened every time I spoke.

'The woman next door told me they were kicking you on the ground,' Pat said.

'Didn't she call the police?' I shivered at the scene my imagination conjured up.

'Of course — but you know how long they take.' Long enough obviously for me to have hobbled all the way out of the scheme — or at least as far as they could be bothered to search for me.

'I don't ever want to set foot in the place again,' I told Pat. He nodded.

'I've already moved some of your stuff back to Wood-haven. I didn't tell them about your being beaten up though.'

'How were they?'

'Improved. At least they're talking about it now.' He laughed. 'Your mother said, "Don't they sometimes change when they get older?" I told her she'd been watching too many American soap operas.'

I hoped that was the truth, but it sounded uncomfortably like a story Pat had invented to cheer me up.

'I've taken all my stuff back to my mother's too,' Pat said. 'Barrowfield was an experiment which failed.' As he said that he lifted his hand from the bedsheet where it had been pressing on mine.

Maurice and 'Lucy' — a new camp friend — came to visit the next day.

'We got sprayed with paint and chased down the street!' Maurice said excitedly, relating the story of how he and his transvestite pals were chased by a gang of youths which had been waiting outside one of the pubs.

'You'll understand if I don't share your enthusiasm for being attacked in the street,' I said, dabbing at my bloody mouth.

Lucy, in full drag, presented me with a bouquet of flowers and a coy smile.

They both left together, chattering about some night out they had arranged. One of the nurses was looking out of the window: no doubt Maurice and Lucy's gang of TVs was awaiting them outside. The way Maurice had reacted to the gay scene was a total surprise to me. It was amazing how little I knew my old pal, despite the years we had spent in each other's company supposedly being intimately revealing.

Pat picked me up from the hospital when they finally let me out after two weeks. It was exhilarating walking the busy Glasgow streets again, especially so near to Christmas. But I was as weak as the doctors had predicted (and I had refused to believe) I would be. The jostling crowds seemed to become thicker and more frenetic the closer we got to the bus station. Entire extended families were thrusting their way through the streets, noisily and self-ishly steamrollering everything in their paths as they did so.

'Breeders!' Pat shouted indignantly.

'Haven't you ever wanted children?' I asked him, only half-jokingly, remembering my unusual despair at the swimming baths — an experience which seemed unfathomable now that my normal healthy impatience with super-straight society had returned.

'Anybody can make a baby,' Pat said very loudly as a huge pregnant woman umbrellaed him off the kerb. 'One wank — that's all it is in the end.'

'Surely a tad cynical, Pat,' I reprimanded.

'It's a biological event,' he said, louder and more dogmati-cally, as though he were drunk, 'no more or less miraculous than any other incident in nature.'

He pointed to two excited children holding hands with their happily indulgent father. 'That's the miracle,' he said. 'It's what the parent does with the child once it's there — the relationship that's created.' He turned to me, lowering his voice. 'Love is the miracle.'

We were approaching one of the pubs that I recognized as 'mixed' from my early days on the scene.

'Let's duck in here for a rest,' I suggested. 'I'm not exactly in a hurry to return to Lanarkshire.'

We drank a Malibu toast to my speedy recovery.

'Although I don't want to go back to Woodhaven,' I said to Pat eventually, 'I do want a home.' During the two weeks I'd lain in hospital, I'd been thinking.

'I've met someone,' Pat said undramatically, rendering obsolete the remainder of my carefully prepared proposal. A crowd of revellers in the pub suddenly burst into a Christmas carol which quickly fizzled out again.

I opened my mouth to speak then closed it again. We both laughed. 'What's he like?' I finally managed to get out.

'Nothing like you!' Pat said, smiling in case I took that the wrong way. 'I only met him a month ago — but I felt that instant something. I always do.'

'You'll always give it a try, won't you,' I said. 'I admire that.'

He seemed to be as embarrassed as I was about the formality that was already creeping into our conversation. We both began to glance around the pub, eager for distraction. At the table next to us I recognized a crowd from the pubs, some of them friends of Alex. There was a young woman with them who I hadn't seen before — was it Diane? She certainly looked the right age; but she was so slim and snug looking that it was difficult to believe that she could recently have given birth. And where was the baby — being looked after by Alex? The thought hurt — but it was a dull ache on a wound that I knew was going to heal up.

The men were all very drunk and talking too loudly — about Alex.

'Alex needs confrontation — a normal relationship bores him.'

'It was the lies I got fed up with.'

'He just fed off all my insecurities.'

'Your insecurities — what about his!'

'He always made it so obvious when he was getting fed up with you: towards the end he kept saying to me, "Do you realise that's five weeks I've been seeing you now?"'

The young woman listened to all their tales of woe in silence. She was probably thinking the same thing I was: Towards The End of what? This 'what' did not seem to be a cause of anxiety to Alex's rejects. It seemed to be enough for them that they had spent time with him going through the motions of a relationship, the success of which they competitively measured (I had heard all the stories before) in weeks and months, kisses and orgasms.

'Don't you worry, Diane hen,' one of them said to the woman, 'Alex'll never leave you.'

'He doesn't have to, dear,' another muttered to the table.

Diane said nothing. There was a guilty silence for ten seconds until she took pity on the others and plucked a cigarette from the packet in front of her. Three lighters were instantly flashed in her face, the warm flames dancing on perfect cheek bones. She was beautiful: she could have had anyone.

The conversation round the table was all for her sake. Despite Alex's friends' state of inebriation, their talk was conducted with one eye, physically and figuratively, on Diane. Some of these men were so wounded by Alex that they were still seeking to revenge themselves on him through her: she would carry the bitter message back to him: we know you for what you are; you may have fooled us at the time but we're doing fine now without you.

After three short puffs on the cigarette Diane put it out. (The others watch helplessly; there is a dim echo of the old panic: have I gone too far? He always seems to be one step ahead.) She wouldn't put up with this unless she was getting something out of it too. Diane was satisfying herself that none of these could ever have been a replacement for her — none of these people whom Alex had taunted and threatened her with.

I could see them both, Alex and Diane, face to face in the middle of the tightrope, the rest of us lying bruised and stunned beneath it.

I was embarrassed when I finally turned away from the table to find that Pat had been staring at me.

'I've got to meet John,' he said, and we left before any of Alex's friends recognized me.

I convinced Pat that I would make it safely to the bus station on my own after we'd made optimistic promises to keep in touch, but I was still happy to catch him watching me as I hobbled through the streets and disappeared into the crowd.

Outside the bus station I paused at a newsagent's, overcome by its little home-made Christmas display which, for all its amateurishness, overshadowed all the big department stores' three-storey high, lavishly decorated contraptions. One could see all the care and attention that had gone into it. But the display was faulty: the strong, solid blues, greens and reds of the Christmas lights would periodically shatter and fragment into hazy purples, browns and greys. The bright, solid primary colours reminded me of the flashing strobe-faces at St James' disco the night I saw Jim and Walter 'together' for the first time. But that seemed like three lifetimes ago. I realised now that all the simple emotions burning in those coloured faces were far more complicated, made up, like the display, of a myriad of minor, malleable components.

Pat had already found someone else. That was a shock. He had depended on me less than I had supposed. Or he was better at playing the game than me — or had he realised that there was more than one game. Pat had never planned and calculated and waited for the Next Move — as though life were a game of chess and human beings pawns with only a limited range of moves. Pat had grabbed at life with both tiny, pink hands — and he was already reaping the benefits. Where had all my careful, calculated risks brought me now? The road back home.

I glanced over into the bus station: my bus was quietly growling, resting before it would lazily coil out of the station and wind its way out of the city. My seat at the back was warm, but how long would it take to escape this time?

I went inside the newsagent's, bought an evening paper, glanced over the ads for another home in another city. Up close, I could see what was wrong with the Christmas display: every now and then one of the circuits of light glowed too brightly, overpowering the other, which dimmed and flickered precariously, threatening to blow out the whole thing. But when both burned with equal intensity all the coloured lights merged into one vibrant fusion which radiated all the colours of the imagination.

When I looked back from a distance, the sun down, the world darker and colder, the lights glowed brighter and stronger than ever.